Lucky Drummer
From NYC Jazz to Johnny Carson

by Ed Shaughnessy
with Robyn Flans

© 2012 Ed Shaughnessy

ISBN 978-1-888408-16-4

REBEATS PUBLICATIONS
219 Prospect, Alma, Michigan 48801
www.Rebeats.com

Cover design, index, gear diagrams by Rob Cook
Discography typing by Nancy Stringer

Printed in the United States of America

"Whether shouldering the weight of swinging big bands like Oliver Nelson, Duke Ellington,Count Basie, or Jimmy Smith.... or spending over four decades guiding & coaching young drummers; Ed Shaughnessy has been a most respected voice in our music.He is an artist who has made Historic & Vital contributions to jazz."
John Clayton. (Clayton-Hamilton Band, Univ.S.Calif.)

"Ed Shaughnessy is one of my all-time favorite drummers!"
Buddy Rich

" For six decades,Ed Shaughnessy has been a role model for me and countless other drummers. His artistic sensibility, amazing versatility and innate sense of swing has kept him at the top of our profession. I still check out his records.......I am a FAN."   *Peter Erskine*

"Ed Shaughnessy is drum history. He continues to be one of the most knowledgeable & inventive drummers ever. He & Buddy Rich control a big band in the very best manner. After 30 yrs. of playing together, it is always a treat due to his deep roots, vast experience & profound sense of swing.....that's what makes him so special."
Bruce Paulson (Doc S.Band,B.Rich band)

"What a treat to re-live Ed Shaughnesssy's wonderful life in music,from his early days as a big band fan through his first meetings with so many jazz immortals. I love this book."
Leonard Maltin

Where it's at....

I was a sixteen-year-old pimply-faced kid, walking the streets of Greenwich Village, carrying a snare drum and a pair of brushes. I was so naïve, but naiveté works well sometimes. I had never really played in New York, except at Manny's Music Store. I passed an open door of a little club called the Village Corner, and a booming voice came from a good-looking, beautifully dressed black man: "Hey young man, where are you going with that snare drum?" I said, "I'm looking for a place to play." He said, "Why don't you come in here and play with us."

This was George Duvivier, who later became, you might say, the Ray Brown of New York, one of the greatest bass players in the history of jazz. He's ten years older than me, and at that time he had a King Cole-like trio— guitar and bass and piano but no drums. The trio would let me come there two nights a week with my little snare drum— they got me a stool, and it was great; they played really good. This was my first experience with real musicians. It was probably my first experience with black musicians— just think of the kindness of George Duvivier. Ten and fifteen years later, he and I became one of the most hired rhythm sections in recorded New York history, alongside Milt Hinton and Osie Johnson on drums. So that's the story I'm about to tell.

MY CHILDHOOD

I was an only child. My parents were Tom and Theresa Shaughnessy. My dad was a longshoreman who worked on the docks in New York. My mom sometimes worked in the sewing factory. I grew up in downtown Jersey City, New Jersey, across from City Hall, in a blue-collar area. It was mostly populated by families who were Irish, German, Italian, Polish, and Russian, and maybe an occasional Jewish family, like my friend Marty, who lived not too far away. There wasn't a black soul to be seen.

Everyone on my mother's side of the family played piano. In those days, there wasn't television, so listening to the radio and playing piano and singing songs with the family were big parts of the social interaction. My mother's brother, Uncle Harry Geetlein, was an engineer and the only one in the family with a college education. He had an engineer's job with Bell Laboratories, and I really looked up to him. He was also a part-time bandleader. He had a little seven- or eight-piece group that would play for dances. I only heard them once or twice because he lived quite far away from us, but I liked him a lot. He was a really terrific guy.

My father was what I would call a "kindly alcoholic," meaning he wasn't abusive, but any alcoholic is a problem. My uncle, whom I only saw a few times a year, was really a better role model for a young boy. I loved my dad, and he was a good man, but he also was a very involved alcoholic, meaning he wasn't home most nights. Good man that he was, however, he brought me my first two drums, toting them on the subway from New York. A guy owed him twenty bucks but couldn't pay, so he said, "Doesn't your son like music?" And the guy gave my dad the drums instead of the money. My dad brought home a bass drum in kind of a case, and a snare drum and a pedal—the most rudimentary things you could think of. I was fourteen and had never expressed any interest in playing the drums. I had played piano, but fate intervened. I set up the little drum set in the basement. I think it took me a day and a half to set it up, even though it was only a bass drum, a snare drum, and a dinky little cymbal.

1

At age twelve I started taking piano lessons—everybody was supposed to play the piano in those days. Although we lived in the blue-collar district of Jersey City, everybody in my family had to take piano lessons. I really didn't like the piano lessons that much, but being a good son, I went—although half reluctantly. My teacher was Miss Martha, who was pretty and nice, and I took lessons from her for about two years. Then, all of a sudden, my dad brought me home those drums, and my attention could not stay on the piano. I asked to stop taking lessons.

As soon as the drums came into the house, I got fired up and I started listening to late-night radio broadcasts of Count Basie, Woody Herman, and Duke Ellington. These were live remote broadcastings from hotels and night-clubs, and I really got the jazz bug. I would play my funny little drums along with the music.

I was a paper delivery boy—if I wanted to have something, I earned money for it. I delivered my papers, saved my money, and then went over to Silver and Horland in New York, which was the big store we all knew about in Jersey, and I bought my first cymbal. I would just sit and play it—ching, ching, ching. That sound of that cymbal compared with that dinky thing. I just had a feast of sounds. I kept delivering papers and kept saving for things like a cheap hi-hat stand and cheap cymbals.

Within six months of my having the drums, I saw the movie *Blues in the Night*, the great classic movie from 1941, with Billy Halop as the drummer, and I thought he was it. He was a dynamic, good-looking guy. The movie was about a jazz band that traveling around and was really broke, but it gave me a sense of camaraderie, even though I didn't have anybody but me and the drums at the time. I watched it a few months ago, and it's still so great. Billy Halop was such an inspiration to me, and it was a good time for me to see that movie.

I was a Boy Scout and my scout master, Joe Ryder, who was a great guy, was a marching drummer. I asked him to give me some lessons—he didn't have a drum set, but it was a way to get started. At age fifteen or sixteen, my very best friend Kenny O'Brien, who first played clarinet, switched to bass, and we practiced together in my basement. I was later able to get him a job with Charlie Ventura when we were eighteen. In later life I really appreciated that I'd had such a good buddy, whose fanaticism for music was just like mine. We'd both get up at 4:00 in the morning, and start out on the subway for New York, with a sandwich in a brown bag, so that we would be first or second in line at the Paramount to see a band. We'd stand in the winter cold, sometimes for two hours, so we'd get a good seat and never thought anything but "Ain't this great!" We'd get there at 6:00 a.m., they'd open the doors at 8:00, and they'd start the first show at 9:00. We'd stay for three or four shows—we'd know that frickin' movie really good!

The pièce de résistance was we went to see Gene Krupa at the Capital Theater. Gene Krupa did a great show. He brought out two white timpani, and

2

he played a symphonic piece on the timpani, and then he played on the drum set. We thought that was the greatest—we stayed for two shows. The movie shown at the Capital when Gene played there was *Since You Went Away*, about WWII veterans. The movie ran two hours and twenty minutes, and with the the fill-in extras and the news, we had to wait close to three hours in between each stage show. One of us would go pee while the other watched his seat. And we'd eat our bagged sandwiches—it was a great time. All that waiting—we didn't care about the movie— was worthwhile when that band came up in the orchestra pit and the light went on.

Four years later, I was sitting up on the drums with Tommy Dorsey's band when Buddy Rich had left. The stage went up for the first time and Dorsey began to play the theme, and the hair on my neck stood up because I had sat on the other side of the stage. I thought, "Boy, you are one lucky guy. Four years ago, I was watching; today, I'm sitting up here."

One of my favorite places to go during my teenage years was the Café Rouge in the Hotel Pennsylvania, down at 33rd Street. This was really a treat—I'd take the subway for ten cents from Jersey City and would get off at 33rd Street. Then after I walked through a long tunnel, the Hotel Pennsylvania was right there. As usual, I'd wear my good confirmation suit with a shirt and tie. I tried to look like a neat, young teenager—and hoping to look older than I was, of course. I found out I could stand outside of the velvet rope in front of the Café Rouge, where I wasn't in anyone's way, and nobody ever bothered me—they were very nice. I think they knew I was there to hear the music. I could see the band quite clearly, straight ahead of me, and hear it, too. That's where I went to hear Les Brown's band, with the wonderful Dick Shanahan. I went a lot of times to hear the '44–'45 edition of Woody Herman's band, with the great Davey Tough on drums. I had been listening to him for close to two years on the radio on "remotes," which were radio broadcasts from hotels and nightclubs around the country. That was a great for the jazz listener. I had to stay up a little late at night to listen, which I did by putting my radio under the covers in bed. I'd hear Davey just swinging his butt off with Woody's band. When I finally got to see him for the first time, there was this little guy, who looked like he weighed 95 pounds. He was small and frail-looking, yet he was driving with a Mack truck power, and he made great big, flowing motions with his arms when he played—very loose, about as loose as you could imagine a drummer playing. I was so thrilled to death to finally see this vision of rhythmic intensity. I got friendly with him, and he was so nice to me. He took me down to his house in Greenwich Village, gave me a couple of intellectual magazines (because he was an intellectual) and told me what would be good to read—the Partisan Review and things like that. He was just so very friendly and helpful. He had an abstract sense of humor and was a great writer. He would have written great stuff if he had lived longer.

We really didn't talk too much about drums. He liked to talk about lit-

3

erature and other things. I met his lovely little wife, Casey. I would go to Café Rouge three times a week when Woody and Davey were there for a couple of weeks. They would play something that would last maybe ten minutes, like "Flying Home," and they would be swinging so hard. I was so impressed that I finally snuck over by the bandstand on a couple of nights, and when the musicians walked off the bandstand, little Davey was still sitting there wiping himself off—he was soaking wet with sweat—and as they went by him, almost every musician said, "That was great, Davey," and it made such an impression on me because he didn't play a note of solo drums. He played what was more important—a great rhythmic foundation for that band.

Boy, I'll tell you, no one could swing harder in a big band than Davey. It was just uplifting to hear. It was a selfless sort of thing. He was only concerned for the group, with what he could contribute to the band. They respected him so much that his nickname was Jesus Christ (seriously, that was his nickname), meaning he could do no wrong, and that's how everyone looked up to him. It was a great, great listening experience. He used to let me sit in once in a while on 52nd Street. He was another example of the older, friendly drummer who had a lot of heart and patience for younger guys like me.

Davey was a great guy, a wonderful guy, and he was very kind to me—very encouraging—and he let me play every once in a while. But he was a terrible drinker. He fell and hit his head while intoxicated, and died at age 41. It was very tragic; it was a shame. My idol, Sidney Catlett, also died early, at age 41, but he didn't bring it on himself. He liked to stay up and party a lot, but as far as I know, he wasn't known as a big drinker. He died of a heart attack while at the theater. We lost those two guys much too soon. Both were wonderful drummers and great guys, and they both treated a young guy like me so very, very well. Big Sid Catlett would see me over in the nightclub. By the time he noticed me about the fourth time, he said to me, "You a drummer?" And when I answered, "Yes, sir," he said, "I think we'll have you play a tune."

Oh, my God! It was Ben Webster on saxophone; Erroll Garner, who became one of the world's most famous pianists, on piano; and a great bass player named John Simmons. Big Sid had me get up there and play two tunes with them—I was only seventeen! They all told me that I sounded good, but I think they might have been lying.

THE GOOD OL' DAYS–
THE STAGE-SHOW ERA

I started going to stage shows when I was fourteen or fifteen, which puts it about 1944. At that time, we had the Paramount Theater, the Strand Theater, the Capital Theater, and Loew's State all going at the same time. Each presented a movie and a show, all year, seven days a week. Loew's State didn't have the biggest acts, but that's where I first saw Louie Jordan's absolutely sensational little big band, and Louie Jordan sang, "Is You Is or Is You Ain't My Baby." That was his big record. The theaters presented a stage show, which was a variety show that usually featured a big band, so it would be Tommy Dorsey, and as a very excellent guest star, it would be Tony Martin, the singer, and maybe a great dance act, like Buck and Bubbles.

One of the reasons I did well in that field was that I played a very good show. That helped me a lot, because besides playing with the band, I had to play new music with the acts all the time. The band acted as the back-up for all of the acts, so I had to be a good reader and show drummer. It was a lot of fun. I have always enjoyed pretty much all aspects of show business. I enjoy playing for a good tap dancer, with good timing and good steps. I even enjoy playing for jugglers, even though they're the hardest to play for because you have to keep the band together by the drumbeats with your feet, while drumming with your hands to catch the tricks—and they're never in time. Jugglers throw a ball in the air and catch it, and it never comes out in rhythm. So the secret, which I'm giving publicly for the first time now, is to keep the band together with your feet and catch all the abstract things with your hands. Many drummers screw up when they play with a juggler, because they try to do everything with the tricks, and the band goes bye-bye. They don't keep the band together enough because they're concentrating on the act.

It was a great era; it was a time when the crowd wasn't turned over—they could stay through to the next show. Once, as a member of the audience, I stayed for four Woody Herman shows. I remember the stage coming up from below the floor, and he was playing "Blue Flame," very slowly with tom-toms, and the lights would flicker, and the audience went wild. It was very, very glamorous at that time for young musicians. Once the stage was up, the band

5

would start playing something fast, like "Apple Honey," or one of their hits. Oh, it was exciting. I can even feel the excitement, just writing about it now. If you were a music nut, you were in seventh heaven. And it was a great chance to study drummers. Just think about it: at my age, I couldn't go to a nightclub (although I did sneak into a few). But a stage show was legit, and you could really watch and listen to a drummer on a stage—as well as get a good bunch of studying done during two or three shows.

The band sometimes did five shows a day. When I was at the Apollo with Charlie Ventura, I did six shows a day. Television killed the stage shows. People started staying home when they began to see variety shows like the Ed Sullivan Show. But the stage-show era was a great time. You could go to four to six jazz clubs on 52nd Street and not spend more than a dollar or two to have a beer and listen to all these great players—four clubs within a block! I feel bad today for the younger musician who won't have that experience.

SUNDAY JAMS

On Sunday afternoon there were jam sessions in New York City, put together in ad hoc style. It was fascinating—there would be Ben Webster playing sax, and Dizzy Gillespie playing trumpet, and maybe Max Roach on drums or Specs Powell, from the earlier era, on drums. The whole thing was fascinating, and you heard some freshly made jazz music, which is what my good buddy Kenny and I would go over to New York to hear. We'd go over on the ferry or take the subway and then take one of the local trains up or walk up to 52nd Street and the surrounding area. Most of the sessions would be held in small ballrooms. Monty Kay and a guy named Mal Braverman would rent them and run the sessions; they did a good job. A lot of people liked the Sunday afternoon sessions because they didn't like to go out late at night. And another advantage of these Sunday sessions was that there were no concerns with people drinking too much or the cops having to intervene, like there were at a nighttime thing. The Sunday sessions were so very relaxing, but they were also valuable.

One valuable lesson I learned from these jam sessions was the fast-tempo lesson. There were a bunch of guys on the stand with a drummer (who shall remain nameless—not a big-name drummer but moderately.) Whoever was in charge of the tunes beat a rather fast tune. It became apparent after the first chorus or two that the drummer couldn't keep up. He was scuffling and not keeping the time, and everybody seemed kind of unhappy. So they called an end to the tune, and they called for Specs Powell, who was in the house, to come up. Specs came up, sat down, and really took care of business. They started another tune at about the same tempo, and Specs just sat there like he was driving a Rolls Royce. It made a great impression upon a young drummer of about sixteen that one of the requisites, if you want to make it with the big boys, was fast tempos that were especially popular at that time.

Because of the advent of the be-bop guys like Charlie Parker, Dizzy Gillespie, and Bud Powell, they played everything that was fast and even faster, like "Cherokee" and "I Got Rhythm" and a few other things. I went home from that particular jazz session and practiced even harder on my fast tempos, which I already had been practicing. But boy, that drove the lesson home when Specs sat down and took care of business and was very admired for doing so.

7

The other fellow didn't look very good to everybody because he wasn't up to it. In fact, to be quite honest, he shouldn't have sat in. If you're not up to the level of the other players, you shouldn't sit in. Believe me, the word goes out when you do it great, and the word goes out when you don't do it great.

Another lesson I learned at these jam sessions was how these drummers, like Specs Powell, Max Roach, and Kenny Clarke—these superior drummers—minutely adjusted their playing for each individual artist. If you're playing behind Ben Webster, you don't play the same way as you would play behind Dizzy. If a bop player like Roach played behind Ben Webster, he would play a little bit straighter, as he would behind Charlie Parker. I noticed all the drummers were musical and hip enough to adjust to the style of the player, and that was as valuable a lesson as the fast tempo lesson. Always listen to the soloist, and tune into the soloist's style. That doesn't mean you keep shifting styles like a chameleon; it is just a slight adjustment. You might play fewer accents behind a more mainstream swing player than you would behind a be-bop type player. It's a minor adjustment but an important one, and it makes a drummer compatible when he's playing with players of different styles in a same situation or job.

Specs Powell was an eminent drummer in New York City. He was one of the rare black musicians who had been hired by a staff orchestra—CBS staff orchestra—and the hiring guy, who was very democratic and liberal, was Lou Shoobe. That might have been in the late '40s. He was a pioneer, along with Frank Vaniogne at ABC, for first hiring black players. Specs Powell was extremely good at just about everything. He not only played superb drum set and had played with Red Norvo and Benny Goodman and a laundry list of eminent people, but he was also a very good mallet player—better than I, that's for sure—and he played very good timpani. I think he played piano also. He was a musical guy all over, and he could sit down and play with any of these great big staff orchestras, better than most. When I went on staff in the early '50s, he taught me a lot of things. He'd sometimes have a short temper, but that was okay. He'd say, "Are you going to get ready with the maracas when you have two bars, or are you going to wait until the last beat?" I thought that was kinda cute.

THE TEEN YEARS

I was in the school orchestra with Miss Crystal, who always encouraged me and even gave me a key to the music room, so I could practice with the timpani any time I wanted. After school I could go in and practice for one to two hours, and for a high school kid, that was incredible. I learned about timpani at a very young age. I learned about tuning and intervals, which was really good. The timpani is a musical instrument with pitches and intervals, which opens the drummer's head up to more than racky-dicky-dacky. You start thinking a little more melodically.

I skipped two grades—second grade and seventh grade—so I was a junior in high school when I was only fourteen. I graduated only a few months after my sixteenth birthday. At about fourteen, I met a lovely guy named Willie Sharp at a drum store. He was in the navy, and he said I should get a drum set teacher. I told him there really wasn't anybody in Jersey City who could teach drum set, so he said, "I'm in the navy, and I'm going to be shipping out. Why don't you take my spot with the great Bill West in New York?"

Bill West was one of the two great teachers—it was Bill West and Henry Adler. I said, "Oh boy, how much would that cost?"

He said, "I don't think he would charge you more than about three dollars." I said I thought I could do that. At the time, I was still delivering papers.

It took me about three busses to get to Willie's house. He had his drum set in the living room, and he and his dad would polish that drum set like a Rolls-Royce. He would let me sit at that great drum set. He wasn't really teaching me; he just wanted me to feel good. It meant a lot to me, especially the devotion between the father and the son. I lost track of Willie through the years. I feel bad about that, because it was just out of the goodness of his heart that he suggested that I take his place with his teacher.

Going to Bill West meant a great deal; he was top level. He was a friend of Gene Krupa's—I even met Gene Krupa. All the drummers came up to buy their cymbals from him, and it was a giant leap for a kid like me. I started to sneak into the nightclubs to hear the great jazz players when I was fifteen or sixteen, and there was so much kindness from the older players back then, and it was completely race-free. It didn't matter if you were a white boy from Jersey or a black boy from wherever. Musicians, both black and white, seemed to welcome the young players.

I'm 90 percent self-taught, but I had Bill West for about a year and a half, and he taught me how to read music. And then again, when I say I'm pretty much self-taught, I can't forget that people like Louie Bellson gave me innumerable tips, just as a fine teacher would give me, as well as other fine drummers who did the same. So I'm self-taught to a degree but with a lot of help along the way. Shelly Manne was very helpful. He played fantastic brushes. I'd say, "How do you do that?" And he'd answer, "Well, I come in kind of sideways to get a little thicker sound on the drum." Ah! That was why he sounded different from most guys. That tip was worth a million dollars: play sideways. I became a pretty good brush player with tips like that. I used to go down to listen to Shelly with Stan Kenton, wearing my confirmation suit. That's why they didn't bother me and kick my ass out. I looked presentable.

I didn't have a car, so my father built me a wooden wagon with a high handle to fit the drum set in, and I would push it to my first gigs, which were up to two miles away. (Guys would say, "Hire the kid with the wagon.") When I got there, I would chain the wagon to a light pole. I was just happy to have the gig and make five dollars. I had one or two gigs a month. One was at a strip club, which I thought was really cool—boom, checka-boom, checka-boom.

My dad did what he could, and when he was a little straight, he took me to a ball game or to a wrestling match, but he was just too involved with his problem. There were some acts of kindness, but his problem finally did get to be too much. No one was sleeping at night, because he would be wandering around, loaded and smoking—he set a chair on fire two times and I had to put it out with water. He would sit in the chair, fall asleep, and drop his cigarette. I thought we were all going to burn to death. Finally, when I was about fifteen, I went to my mom—which was so hard to do—and said, "Mom, it's either him or me. I can't go to school and do my work because I'm not getting any sleep." It wasn't that I hated my father; I hated how we were living. We were up almost the whole night with him, and that would cause me to fall asleep in school.

So my mom told him he had to move out, and he got himself a rented room. I felt terrible, but the peace of mind in the house from the first night he wasn't there was unbelievable. We'd gotten used to dealing with him, but it was very exhausting. It was peace and quiet after that.

BILL WEST

Studying with Bill West wasn't just hooking up with a fine drum teacher; it was hooking up with the New York scene, because everybody knew Bill West, and Bill West knew everybody. In a sense, it was an open door to learning to do some networking with some other drummers in New York and with other people. It generally gave me a chance to just get used to New York—I was still the country bumpkin from Jersey. When I came to Bill's for the very first time, I thought it was really glamorous. His studio was on the third floor of a building on 47th Street and Broadway. Actually, his studio was over a dance hall. This was about 1944, and I was fifteen. There was no elevator in the building, so I had to walk up three flights. As I did, I passed the window for the dance hall, which I thought was rather glamorous, because the girls were dancing there. Sometimes a couple of them would come up to visit Bill; they were very colorful. Some of them would do cartwheels, and for young teenage musicians, this was really exciting stuff—it was the big time for a bumpkin from Jersey.

Going up to Bill's, I also met a lot of people who visited him, some as eminent as Gene Krupa, who was a friend of Bill's; the great Louie Bellson; Davey Tough; and I think I met Jo Jones up there once. A lot of great drummers came up there to say hello because Bill had a fine reputation as a teacher, and he was also a very good drummer, a fine player. He could always sit down at a little set of drums that he kept in his place and demonstrate things with a really fine musical touch. He had played with Claude Thornhill's band earlier in the '40s, and now he was in the Merchant Marines, but he did have Saturday off to teach—this was during World War II.

Bill had a lot of stuff going for him. He had a great ear for cymbals, and he sold cymbals. He didn't have a place big enough to have a drum set in stock, but he would order it for you. I learned from him at a very young age what a good ride cymbal is, what a good crash cymbal is, and what a good set of hi-hats should sound like. He let me pick out cymbals for people because he said I had a very good ear. But of course, I really had learned from him. Going up to Bill's was a great move for me. I started getting more familiar with the New York City scene and started to hear about different things, like some of the jam sessions. Certainly, if I had just sat over in Jersey, I would never have gotten in touch with any of that stuff.

That's also where I heard about playing on Saturday mornings above Manny's Music Store on West 46th Street, sometimes called Music Row because there were a lot of music stores. Manny gave this opportunity to young guys to play a jam session up above the store in a big picture window, which was really fun—except all we could play was a snare drum with brushes, so we wouldn't bother the store downstairs. We brought our own brushes, and Manny's supplied the snare drum and the stool. They had a small electric piano that guys played. Horn players and bass players would come in, and I would sit in and play. I actually got a few little gigs from doing that with other guys my age who thought I sounded okay when I played. It was quite challenging to play like that, but I learned how to do that and to get enough steam going off the brushes and just the snare drum.

Bill was also sort of like a surrogate father to me. After all, I was a guy from a broken home, and I really idolized his lifestyle. He had a lovely wife named Ruth and two little boys. They sometimes invited me to go out to Jones Beach with them, and it was a very good, wholesome family image for me. I really liked being around them. They invited me to dinner sometimes too. They lived in Manhasset, Long Island, in a very nice home. It was very good for me to see a musician who was solidly grounded with a family. He was a good father and husband and very important to me. Later on, when he retired from teaching, I would go in and pick up his mail and take it out to him on the train, and he and Ruth would usually have me stay for supper. I had a very fine relationship with the great Bill West. My little friend Willie Sharp did me such a favor when he hooked me up with him.

ANOTHER MENTOR

When I was twenty-three, another important person for me—in an educational and personal sense—was Morris Goldenberg, known as Mo Goldenberg, who was one of the eminent teachers at Juilliard. He was a wonderful percussionist on all the mallet instruments and timpani. He was allowed to teach a few outside students there. I hooked up with Mo, because at that time in New York, there was a lot of work where you would play drum set 95 percent of the time on a date, but they also would want you to get up and play a little timpani and maybe play a few chords on the vibes or on the bells or glockenspiel. I knew I had to get a little bit of that ability—not a whole lot but a little. If they needed a real great, they'd call Harry Brewer or Phil Krause or one of the great mallet players, but I needed to know the simple things. I had my early piano experience, so I knew the keyboards and some chords, but it was very rudimentary. I thought I'd go up to Mo and get some more experience on the mallets and improve my timpani playing. I had a pretty good ear, so I wasn't a bad tuner, but I could use some tips on technique.

He was a great teacher and a great person. He was very fatherly and very nurturing to his students. For instance, he got me to invest in mutual funds at quite a young age, because he said they're solid, not risky, and they would give me something for the future. Little did I know at the time—even though it wasn't a lot of money; maybe it came to $20,000—but that would be the way I got out of paying alimony to my first wife, and I have Mo Goldenberg to thank for that. They were a solid investment, and he would give advice on things like that. I took lessons with him for three years.

The story I like so much is that Saul Goodman, the great timpanist with the New York Philharmonic, was at the studio next to Mo at Juilliard. Mo told me in later years that Saul had asked, "Why are you teaching that Shaughnessy guy? He's a good young drummer on the way up, and you're teaching him all this other stuff. He's going to end up taking your work away from you."

And Mo replied, "Saul, if a guy has to worry about a student taking his work away from him, then he shouldn't teach. I'm not worried about that. Eddie does his thing, and I do my thing."

And sure enough, ten years later, I was on staff with the *Tonight Show* as a drum set drummer, and Mo was on staff as a percussionist who played all the mallet instruments and timpani and did a lot of symphonic shows. He even played cartoon shows, because he could play those desperately fast things on xylophone. He said, "See, Eddie? There's room for everybody." Mo was very important in my life.

POST-HIGH SCHOOL

I graduated high school in June 1945 at sixteen years old. In order to have a union card in New York, you had to have New York residency, so I took a room on 10th Avenue and took a job at the telephone company as a messenger boy. I made a drum pad out of silent sponge rubber so I could practice in my down time in my little work cubicle.

DIDN'T MAKE THE CUT

My first professional job at age seventeen was at the prestigious Hotel Pennsylvania for Randy Brooks—and I got fired because I wouldn't cut my hair. I said, "I won't cut my hair for anybody. Am I here to drum or here for hair?" He was a military type; he wanted short, buzzed hair. When I refused to do it, he fired me. He was going out on the road, which would have been good, but I didn't feel like compromising because he was kind of a stiff guy anyway. Then I got lucky, because I'd played with him—that's the way it always goes. Some musicians had heard me play with him and thought I was okay, and I got another job—my first on the road. And I left the phone company.

BOBBY BYRNE AND THE BIG EASY

Bobby Byrne was an excellent trombonist, and New Orleans was a fascinating place to go to, especially for first-time visitors. There was so much music, and I got great, great experience there, playing ice shows—they're kind of like a circus on ice; everything is fast. The music is fast, the segues are fast—it's one tune into the other. And I thought, "This is perfect for me now," because I'd only played a couple of little local shows before that. I knew what to do, and I had become a good reader. Big Sidney Catlett had been kind to me and said, "Become a good reader, and you'll be able to play shows when there's no jazz work," and that's what I did. I was a good reader and I could play the show, but I was a rather naïve kid. I was into Catholicism at the time. I had not yet had sex, and a couple of the girls from the ice show were coming on to me. I got so nervous that I didn't go out with any of them.

I was staying in a rooming house, right in the heart of New Orleans, and the saxophone player in the room next to me had a different chick in his room every night. They were carrying on … and I was sweating. It was hot and humid, and I'd be listening to "Ah, baby. Ah, do it baby," and wondering why I had to have a room right there. I tried to get another room on another floor, but there weren't any. Oh God, sometimes the girls would moan, and I would wonder what he could be doing. Mr. Naïve. I think back to that and laugh now.

The rumor was that one of the lead ice skaters—a gorgeous blonde girl with blue eyes—was nursing a broken heart because Jimmy Dorsey's band had played there six months ago, and the lead saxophone player had become her lover—she said he had spoiled her for the rest of her life. I, in my naïve state, thought, "Now what did he do that made him so unforgettable?" That's the truth.

So here I was in New Orleans, getting great experience playing shows, being nervous and not knowing what to do around pretty girls who were coming on to me, and suffering with listening to my friend Bernie next door, the great lover. I was glad when the gig was over, just because of the nighttime thing. But in the meantime, I went around and heard a lot of great New Orleans music in the clubs. They played traditional jazz, of course; not be-bop or modern stuff, but they were playing great in that style. And I was thrilled to death to hear a drummer by the name of Monk Hazel, who could play drums with the right hand and coronet with the left hand, or vice versa. I was awed by him. He had a good reputation in New Orleans.

Bobby Byrne, who was the leader of the band in New Orleans, later became a very successful A&R (artists and repertoire) man in New York. I did a lot of work for him in New York, where he would be in the engineer booth as the A&R man.

BACK HOME

After about four months, when we got back, I got a job with Jack Teagarden, who was a traditionalist. He heard me sit in and play a very fast tune with somebody, and he offered me a weekend job. He said, "I like to play fast, but a lot of drummers can't, but you can, can't you?" I said, "Yes, sir, I can." I had practiced at home. While I was coming up, it was the be-bop era. When Charlie Parker and Dizzy Gillespie were doing all this new stuff, they played very fast tempos—"Cherokee" was very fast. So I went out and bought the two fastest records of the time. One was Gene Krupa's "Lover," which I wore out, and the other was faster, by a sax player named Don Byas playing "Cherokee." It was the fastest record I'd ever heard, and I would sit and practice with both those records. I had the weekend with Jack Teagarden, and I was fascinated by the fact that he had a custom-made leather liquor bottle pouch with a chain and a lock. I thought, "This is what the big stars must do." He could leave it in his dressing room, and nobody could get at it. He'd come in the back, and open up the lock and the chain, and take the bottle of booze out of the leather cover, and have himself a taste or two. He was one of those quiet guys and was very nice. I don't want to make it seem that he was a huge drinker, but he probably got tired of people robbing his booze, so he had this custom-made thing. And that made some impression on me! At the time, I was only drinking Coca-Cola.

I also got a job with George Shearing after sitting in with Bud Powell, who was playing solo piano. I got up behind the drums that were there, and he played "Cherokee" for twenty-five minutes, and I stayed with him. Bud Powell did that sometimes. Way before John Coltrane played very long on one tune, Bud Powell did. Anyone who's heard him knows he pre-dated John Coltrane on that. When he had a trio or duo job, he simply would get going, and he could keep playing for twenty minutes. When I did it with him, he didn't have a bass. I don't know where I got the nerve, but I said, "Hey, can I play?" And he grunted, and I sat down, and we started to play. If I hadn't been practicing my ass off on these fast tempos, I never would have made it. That was my open door to the big time. Jimmy Dorsey, the bandleader came up and said, "Do you know you played twenty-five minutes with Bud?" And George Shearing's manager was there and said, "Come over and talk to George," and I got a job for the next week with George.

THE '50s

I had a lot of fun doing experimental music during the '50s. I met Teddy Charles, the vibraphone player, during that time, and he became one of my oldest and dearest friends. We met at a jam session at Nola Studios up on Broadway. There were a great many jam sessions at that time in New York. Teddy and I and a few other guys would chip in something like a buck a piece to rent a studio, like at Nola's famous rehearsal studios, up around 49th Street and Broadway, and we would play together. Teddy and I soon were sharing a second-story pad. He and I would buy a quart of milk and each get a beef stew up at the Horn & Hardart, a popular New York automat. We'd split the quart of milk and eat the beef stew, and that's all we ate all day. When we didn't have enough money, Teddy would put his vibes out on the street and play them with the cover on to attract attention. I'd drum on something like a fire hydrant, and people would come over and give us some money. We'd get enough money to go rent the studio. Once or twice, Miles Davis came up and played with us, which I thought was wonderful. We played kind of a medium-slow song the first time he joined us—this was earlier; it must have been about 1947—and after he got done and packed up, he walked by me and said in his low, gruff voice, "You kept that fuckin' tempo just perfect. Most guys can't play slow that good, you know that?" I said, "No." And he said, "Well, that's the truth. They can play the faster ones, but they don't groove and hold it where they should be. Keep that up." And I thought, "Oh my God, I can go to heaven now." I later became friendly with Miles.

WATCHING FROM THE BALCONY–
WATCHA GONNA BRING?

We had a gimmick: we would charge a quarter or half a buck if someone wanted to come up to our second-story rehearsal room and watch the girls from the Latin quarter change their clothes. The girls left all the windows open, and they'd walk by the windows half-naked (or completely naked) and they couldn't have cared less. We'd make guys bring food, beer, a bottle of wine, or money. We called it "Watching from the Balcony." And I was lucky. The crowd I hung with—Teddy and the guys—were just a beer-and-wine crowd, and that was about it. Nobody we hung with regularly was into heavy drugs or anything. Naturally, I worked with guys who were into that, but the crowd I hung with normally was pretty conservative.

I remember one time, after I had played with Bud Powell once or twice, he asked me to go uptown to a party with him. While I was there, I went to use the bathroom. I opened the door and saw some guy sitting there with a belt around his arm and a great big needle. I'll tell you, I know I sound like Simple Simon, but I'd never seen that before. I got so scared that I ran right out of the place, ran to the subway, and went downtown. I had never seen a junkie shoot up before—he was sitting on the can with a belt around his arm, and it was creepy—and very frightening. I was seventeen at the time, and it made a big impression on me. It really did.

I want to emphasize how very nourishing the New York music scene was in the '50s. Many people think the '50s and some of the '60s were a very golden period in New York music. A lot of the new stuff was happening, but I don't mean it was nourishing just because of that. It's just that you could always get a big band together; often it was Gerry Mulligan, Phil Woods, and me. I belonged to one band named Ronnie Roulier—he was an arranger; he'd get Mulligan, Phil Woods, Clark Terry, and me to all come down and play his music. A lot of these guys had pretty high profiles, and they'd come and play the parts. There was no snobbery at all. That period was important to me, because that was the atmosphere. If there was good music to be played, guys didn't always put a dollar sign on it. Once in a while, Ronnie Roulier would rent Town Hall and give a concert, and we'd play all the music we had been practicing all year. It would be a fun concert—music for music's sake. I think I got a lot of jobs because I would play for guys who would say, "Hey, I'd like to rehearse some new music. Could you come to play for a while?" And if I wasn't working, I'd take my drums and go do it, and they'd remember that next time they had a record date. A lot of guys were loyal that way. I didn't do it for that reason, but it would come back to me.

CHARLIE VENTURA

Charlie Ventura had been with the Gene Krupa Orchestra and had a

17

very big name. He's almost forgotten today, but at the time, he was a big star with Gene. They would do little trio numbers with just piano, sax, and Gene on drums. I liked the way Charlie played—he was self-taught and was a phenomenally gifted saxophonist. He could play be-bop on the bass sax, which today, I've been told by bass sax players, is impossible, but he used to do it. He played great tenor sax, alto sax, baritone sax, and bass sax. But he was famous for being the tenor sax soloist with Gene Krupa during the mid-1940s. He made his name with Gene Krupa, and I made my name with Charlie Ventura.

Charlie Ventura hired me in 1948. I had sat in with him on 52nd Street, where he was playing with Bill Harris, the great trombonist, who had left Woody Herman and one of my early idols, Davey Tough. Davey, who was a friend of mine, said, "Why don't you play some the next set," so I played a couple of tunes, and later did that another night. And after that, Charlie took me in the back and said, "Ed, I'm getting a new group together. It's going to be very unique. I have Jackie Cain and Roy Kral, who are going to sing sort of be-bop vocalese, and I would very much like you to join the group."

I said, "That sounds very different." And he said, "Oh, it's different. I'm going to have four horns and a rhythm section." In those days we used to call that a "big little band," because four horns wasn't the usual Charlie Parker, Miles Davis group. Most of the combos were four and five pieces, and as soon as it went up to something like four horns and rhythm, it was called the "big little band" or "little big band." I said, "Charlie, I'd love that"—this was in the middle of my eighteenth year.

Jackie and Roy did something that was different from what anyone else had done—mixing the bop syllables in with the lyrics, and from the first gig we did, the band was a sensation. It was very musical and had a lot of great people in the band: Conte Candoli, the great trumpet player—he was only a year older than I at the time; Bennie Green, who was a wonderful and original trombonist and one of the leading lights of the new trombone players; Boots Mussulli on alto, formerly with Stan Kenton and one of my boyhood friends; Kenny O'Brien, who I recommended on bass. Wherever we went, we did stand-out business. It was really fun for a guy like me. I had never been with anything famous before. We headlined at the big theaters in Chicago and all the major cities. We did theaters and some clubs, and we even played sometimes in Chicago's black Southside, which I found a lot of fun, because when the people there liked the music, they really let you know. I think our band was admired equally by blacks and whites. Over the next two years, we were the number-one small band in the country.

Charlie was not only a brilliant musician, but he also was a very kind person—and that was important to a young guy like me. After all, prior to going out with a hot act like this, I only had a few minor band credits. I don't mean that I wasn't confident as a drummer, but Charlie was the kind of guy who would tell me how good I sounded. "Man, you sound so good," he'd say. "You're so good for the band, I love ya." He was like a combination coach, father figure, and fellow musician. I think I played better because of all those qualities that he brought out, because he would say, "Go for it. Go for it, man. You're just doing great." And he would always feature a drum solo for me and give me a good presentation. I can't say enough good things about him. He was a sharp guy. He loved to get custom-made clothes and thought the height of his success was when he had his initials embroidered on his socks. I thought that was very hip, too. I remember when he first showed me—he said, "Eddie, come here a minute," and he picked up his pant leg to show the embroidered "CV" on his socks. And I, the Jersey bumpkin, said, "Charlie, that's got to be the height of it!"

For the first time in my life, I had a few bucks. I loved Sherlock Holmes, so I went to a tailor and had him make me a blue, red, and white houndstooth overcoat for the winter in a Sherlock Holmes style, with the overlapping lapels. It wasn't in bad taste; it was a quiet houndstooth. I felt like it couldn't get much better than that. I had one or two jackets made, too. It was a place where all the bands went for clothes; I think it was called something like Chicago Al's. And there was a place next to the Apollo Theater named Hollywood Al's, where, if you were a hip musician—black or white—you had to go to get your zoot suit pants, and I did. I went from Jersey up to Hollywood Al's and got a pair of light-blue balloon zoot suit pants. When I wore them in Jersey, I almost got stoned—and I don't mean high. People looked at me in such a way that I tended not to wear those pants too often in Jersey. Zoot-suiters had a bad name, generally speaking, to the conservative crowd. But if you could get a pair of pants at Hollywood Al's, that was it!"

A STAR IS BORN

Burt Korall, who wrote *Drummin' Men—The Heartbeat of Jazz: The Swing Years* and *Drummin' Men—The Heartbeat of Jazz: The Be-Bop Years*, wrote in the second book that when I joined Charlie Ventura's band, I became immediately famous. I didn't realize that at the time, but according to Korall, that put me immediately on the map. That would be like today saying a guy named Brian Blade is playing with Wayne Shorter. Everyone knows Brian Blade from playing with Wayne Shorter. When Dave Weckl played with Chick Corea, it immediately put Weckl on the map—then it made sense. Charlie Ventura had the number-one small band in the country at the time. I know it seems naïve, but I didn't realize it until years later he when told me, "We used to say in New York, 'Well, Eddie's famous now.'"

When I got that job with Charlie, I got an endorsement from Slingerland Drums, and I got my first real drum set. When that drum set came, there was no living with me! I'll tell you—it was the greatest! I had designed this drum set. It was sort of a scaled-down Louie Bellson drum set, but my innovation was that I put a bongo drum in the middle of the two tom-toms, and I would play the bongo drum with the left stick while I played the normal cymbal rhythm in jazz. A lot of people liked that when we made records and in concert, because it sounded like we had a percussionist accompanying us sometimes. It's a small thing, but people remember it, even to this day. Ed Thigpen, an old friend of mine, often says, "When are you going to put the bongo back?" It's a double bass, but it follows my little idiosyncrasy of the right-hand drum being 14 inches wide and the left-hand drum being 12 inches, getting two different sounds. That's the only thing I did slightly different to get away from Louie's exact same sound. I just wanted to have a little something of my own.

THE TIME I DIDN'T

I was working at the Royal Roost with Charlie Ventura—this was when the band was very hot—and Ava Gardner came in one night with a group of people. After we played our set, someone brought a note up to me that read, "I'd very much like to meet you. Ava." I had heard she was a pretty active chick, sexually, so I didn't think this was a particularly singular compliment

I said to the waiter, "Tell her I'm busy." I had a very cute girlfriend at the time, and I wasn't interested in boffing Ava Garner. I know a lot of people who use those things as notches on the belt, but that wasn't me. I never did go over to her table. The waiter later told me she got pissed when she got my message and left shortly afterwards. But the guys loved it. "You'll be sorry you turned down Ava Gardner," they told me, and they rode me mercilessly about it.

THE TIME I DID

I was nineteen, at the peak of my popularity at that time, playing at the Blue Note with Charlie Ventura. It was standing room only, with lines outside. I loved playing there, because we also stayed at a hotel right across the street. The club owner there really treated the bands with respect. We were in the middle of the engagement—I think it was a busy Saturday night—and the band was very hot. We had played an extra set, so I was very tired and didn't hang out afterwards. I went up to bed and to sleep, but at about 3:00 in the morning, there was pounding at my door. Half asleep, I yelled, "Who is it? Who is it?"

"It's Anita O'Day. Open the door."

"I'm asleep," I called to her.

And she said, "If you don't open the door, I'm going to start screaming."

I had met Anita once, in passing, so I got up and opened the door.

She said, "Let me in! Let me in!" She was either high or loaded; I have no idea which it was. She looked nice, but I said, "I'm sleeping. What do you want?" She was a pretty famous lady by then. She had gone out on her own after singing with Krupa, and I didn't want a big scandal by calling the cops or anything. So I figured, what's she gonna do? She's not going to kill me.

She came in, and I shut the door, and she said, "You really sounded great tonight." I thanked her, and she said, "You know I love drums, don't you?"

I said, "Oh, yeah, I know you love drums."

"I loved working with Gene," she told me. "Great drummer."

I said, "Oh, yes, one of the greatest."

She said, "I have to be satisfied tonight."

"Huh?"

"I have to be satisfied," she repeated. "I'm physically all up and going, and I have to be satisfied, and I'm not leaving until I'm satisfied."

"You're kidding, aren't you?"

"I'm just going to stay here," she said, and she started to take her clothes off. "I'm going to stay here until I'm satisfied, and then you can go back to sleep."

So that's what I did. At nineteen, I was such a greenhorn. I had just started having sex maybe six months before that with my girlfriend, because I was a good Catholic boy and shouldn't have sex—all that ridiculous guilt stuff. I was so scared of cops coming and that I might have to go down to jail if they took Anita that it seemed easier to do what she wanted than to make any trouble. We had a pretty good time, I'll say that. And after she had a cigarette or two, she got dressed, said "Nice night," and left—and I went back to sleep.

The kicker is, forty years later, easily, in the late '80s, I was coming out of LAX with my bag, and Anita was at the corner, where a limo was picking her up. She looked over and said, "Shaughnessy, that was a nice night," and got in the car. I thought it was remarkable that she even remembered the night, because she was feeling pretty good that night, but she did. I stood on the curb and laughed. And I never saw her again after that.

ROAD STORIES

On the way to a gig with Charlie Ventura, somewhere out west—I think we were bound for Denver—we had a terrible auto crash. We were traveling in two cars, with George, the road manager, pulling the drums, the bass, and all the luggage in a little trailer behind his car. The singer Jackie Cain was driving the car I was in, and she fell asleep at the wheel. We hit one of those big stone walls, going quite fast. Her husband, Roy Kral, woke up when he heard her scream, and he tried to protect her, but he went out through the windshield. Almost unbelievably, he only suffered a gash across his forehead. Luckily, a sheriff's car came pretty quickly and got Roy to the hospital quickly.

I almost lost my left eye in the crash. At the time, I thought I had, but I got lucky—I hit it right above the eye. And although Roy was hurt quite badly, within two weeks he was working with us again. Roy felt he was lucky to be here. Don't forget—there were no seat belts in the 1940s. None of us would have gotten hurt half as bad if there had been seat belts.

On the funny side of car traveling, when we got done with a job in Detroit, we were going to have a week or two off. Charlie Ventura said to me, "Hey, Eddie, how would it be if we got to New York by tomorrow?"

I said, "We're in Detroit. You mean, driving your Cadillac?"

"Yeah, we'll burn it up," he said. "We won't sleep."

"Charlie, we already had one accident," I reminded him.

And he said to the greenhorn, here, "I know this thing to do." Not that Charlie would lead anyone down a bad road; he wasn't a druggie guy or anything like that, but he said, "You buy some Benzedrine inhalers"—which can't do today—"and you take the strips out. You soak them in tea, and then you drink it. You never go to sleep right away."

So we did that. We not only drove all the way to New York, but I didn't sleep for another two days. I stayed awake completely, twenty-four hours a day, for three days—I thought I'd go crazy. Obviously, I never tried that again. I asked Charlie if he got to sleep, and he said, "Oh, yeah, as soon as I got home I went to sleep."

I had so many negative experiences with things like that and losing friends to drug overdoses, that, in a way, it was out of fear that I stayed away from a lot of stuff. I can't say I was such a wonderful fellow with high morals, but I got frightened, because when you know people who have died from taking stuff, it's the best thing to keep you away.

While I was on the road with Charlie Ventura, I did have an incident with marijuana. I never was a big grass smoker; I wasn't afraid of it or anything, but I never was into it. Then somebody at a party in Chicago said, "Come on, man, we're all lighting up." So I took a couple of tokes, and then I got behind the drums. Charlie Parker walked in and took his horn out, and we started to play together with a bunch of guys. Somebody made a tape, and when I heard it the next day, I said, "Oh, boy, the weed and I don't get along!" I did not like the drumming at all. I thought Bird sounded fine, but it taught me a good lesson—that weed didn't go well with me. I was having a wonderful time, but I wasn't playing good. That made a big impression on me.

One of the last things we did with Charlie was a terrifically successful concert in Pasadena in early January '49—I wasn't yet twenty years old. We packed the place, and it was the first jazz concert that was put on an LP record. Before that, you had to play four 78s to play a whole concert. Jazz at the Philharmonic was recorded on 78s. The man who did our concert was Gene Norman, a very far-reaching guy, and he said, "Let's use the new technology." Two 12-inch records took up what would have been six 78 rpm records.

The LP was called *Charlie Ventura, Live in Pasadena*. The band broke up about six months later, after working together for about a year and a half, because Jackie and Roy wanted to go out on their own, which was understandable. Charlie tried to reorganize the band with some other voices, but it just couldn't capture what Jackie and Roy had done. Roy had written all the lines, and the two of them could sing together like two fingers on a hand.

THE BIRD KNOWS

When I was with Charlie Ventura in '48 and '49, we often played in New York. The primary job I want to mention was ten weeks in '49 at a very well-known nightclub called the Royal Roost. It was run by a very nice man named Ralph Watkins, and he booked a package of Charlie Parker's Quintet, the Charlie Ventura Group, and Billy Eckstine—three separate attractions. There were lines of people in the street and around the corner, even in the middle of the week. It's probably one of the most successful engagements I've ever been part of. Jazz, particularly the newer jazz, be-bop style, was very popular.

The Royal Roost was a club where you went down the stairs to a basement level. It had kind of a low ceiling, which gave it a much more intimate feeling than a lot of other nightclubs. Ralph had some foliage—leaves and ivy—on the ceiling, and it felt like a fun place. The business was great, the reception was great, and I got a chance to get to know Charlie Parker quite well.

My girlfriend at the time, who was the hat check girl at the club, was quite friendly with Charlie Parker's first wife, Doris. Doris was a lovely girl, and because the two girls were friendly, when my girlfriend would take a break, she would sit with Doris Parker, who was there all night, listening to Charlie. When we weren't playing, I would sit with my girlfriend, and Charlie would sit with his wife in the same booth. We knew each other already—to say hi, as fellow musicians—but I really got to know Charlie in a more personal way.

Although Charlie died from a drug overdose at age 34, when I was with him, I never had the feeling he was stoned. Regardless of whether he was or wasn't, there certainly were no outward signs, as far as I could see. And he was playing great, every set. When I would talk to Charlie, he always was very helpful. He said, "I want you to buy some Stravinsky records, like 'Rite of Spring' and 'Firebird,' because you like odd temps, and Stravinsky is a master of the odd tempos– 5/4, 7/4, 9/4. I want you to see how he moves the tempos in and out."

Charlie was the most eclectic person I'd ever met. Once he told me, "I want to take you uptown sometime to the Hungarian Lunch Club."

"Oh, good food?" I asked.

He said, "Not just good food; they also have a Hungarian swing band with violins and dobros. They swing better than we do." He also would talk about ballet music. He was just a mile wide, and I thought it was fascinating that his interests spanned such a wide area. He was a rare person, whether you

23

played with him or sat in the audience and listened. I would stay in the club to hear his sets a lot of times. I heard a lot of Charlie Parker, especially on a ten-week engagement, but that's how much he impressed me. It was so fresh all the time.

I remember one time he came off stage after playing only two choruses on a song that was thirty-two bars, and I heard someone say to him, "Gee, Bird, you only played two choruses on that tune. Why didn't you play more?" And he looked at the guy and said, "I practice at home." Fascinating man, and he still fascinates today. I've never seen the movie Bird, just because I heard it gives a dark picture of him. It must be true– I don't think Clint Eastwood would direct a movie that wasn't true– but I guess I saw the better side of Charlie Parker.

He also used to sit in at the Café Society downtown with Mundell Lowe and Tony Scott's group. He'd play with us all night, sometimes two nights on a weekend, when he wasn't working. He liked to play all the time, and I got to know him pretty well then. I never made a studio recording with Bird, but I do have a copy of *Charlie Parker & Friends*, a Parrot Records bootleg of us playing at Cafe Society in New York in the early 1950s. Playing with him was great. Sometimes I'd get so fascinated with what he was playing, I'd forget how to play myself. He was always so encouraging and made me feel so good. "Oh, Eddie," he'd say, "you sound so great. Keep it up."

He once said to me, "I like the fact that you're a clean kid, Eddie. Stay that way." And then he told me that the reason he liked the album *Bird with Strings* was that he was cold sober when he made it. I thought it was interesting that maybe he didn't think he always played his best when he was high. Not that I ever heard him play bad—I never did—but that's what he told me. I wanted to repeat the story, because Bird with Strings happens to be my favorite Charlie Parker record, too. He said that probably people wanted to him to say it was his favorite album because he was really high and really blowing, but no, he said, "By the way, the Bird with Strings record was my favorite. I was really straight and cold sober." Somebody once said to me, "Well, you must have seen him at the best times," and I said, "Fine, then, I'll take it."

FIRST TIME IN RECORDING STUDIO

Louie Bellson—another great jazz drummer—and I once rented Nola Studios, paid an engineer, and went in with two bass drums and a snare drum. We did four tunes with lovely names, like "We've Got Bells On"—just drums—and we had the best time. The popular drummer and composer Joe La Barbera said to me once that we had to find those records. I have them hidden away somewhere—they're evidence of the fun things we did at the time.

MEETING LOUIE AND SIR DUKE

Meeting Louie Bellson had a great effect on my life. My teacher Bill

West knew Louie very well, and I said, "Gee, I sure would like to meet Louie Bellson." At this time, I was fifteen years old, and Louie was playing with Benny Goodman at a rather classy place. Bill said, "If you'd like to meet Louie, I'll give you a note."

I went over to the place where he was playing, wearing my same confirmation suit, and I asked the maître d' if he would bring the note to Mr. Bellson. The band was on break, so Louie came out and was so amazing. He said, "Hi, Eddie! You're a student of Bill West? Would you like to hear the band?" And he got me a side table and sat me down. That was the kind of guy he was. He had never met me before and yet he said, "Hey, Eddie, why don't you come over to my hotel on Saturday. I have a little free time, and I want to show you this new technique I'm studying in California."

I quickly responded, "Yes, sir. I'll be there with bells on—no pun intended."

When I went to his hotel, he spent two hours showing me a new finger-control bouncing technique that he was studying, and I thought to myself, "This guy is already one of the biggest names in drumming—really, the first challenge to Buddy Rich that has come along—and how nice is he?"

Every time he was in town I went to see him, and he planted the bug in me to use two bass drums. He sat me down at his drums and said, "You were meant for two bass drums." He was lying through his teeth, I know, but he gave me another pedal and said, "Now you just have to find another old bass drum."

I did find an old beat-up drum at a second-hand store. It didn't look like mine—it wasn't even the same size—but I didn't care. I started practicing my double-bass drum, like Louie. This kindness was something he showed to everyone he came in contact with. He loved sharing and giving of himself.

When Louie got married to Pearl Bailey in 1952, he recommended me to sub with Duke Ellington. I didn't want to take the job. I was only twenty-two years old, so I said, "Louie, maybe in ten more years I'll be ready for Duke."

He said, "Duke knows you, and Duke said if you come, I can take off. He knows you from Charlie Ventura."

I said, "Charlie Ventura is Charlie Ventura. Duke Ellington is Duke Ellington." I agreed to sub, though, because I couldn't say no to him.

I quit after the first night. No tragedies happened; I thought it just wasn't good enough for Duke Ellington. I said, "I'd like to leave tonight, Mr. Ellington."

He said, "Whose band is this?"

I said, "Duke Ellington's." He said, "Who do you think runs this band?"

Again I responded, "Duke Ellington."

"Duke Ellington tells people when they go, and only Duke Ellington," he said. "You don't tell Duke Ellington when you go. You did fine tonight." There was no music for the drummer at the time on the Duke Ellington band. Sonny Greer didn't read music. Louie learned everything from ear. When you were up there playing, sure, you could play "Take the A-Train," but he would pull out the second movement of "Black, Brown, and Beige," which is almost a symphonic piece. He was such a good conductor. I had Clark Terry next to me, telling me what to do, and I got through it okay, but I didn't think I should stay. But he said, "Nobody raises hell in my band the first night. Now, tomorrow night, it'll be better."

And sure enough, it was better. And by the time we'd played a week in Birdland, everybody said it sounded pretty good. I still thought I'd sound better in ten years.

It was quite an experience. Let me tell you how that band functioned. We were playing a big dance in Newark the first night, and I got there about 7:30. The drum set was set up and everything was ready to go. The job started at 8:00. When the bass player, Wendell Marshall, got there, it was just the two of us, nobody else. At two minutes to 8:00, Wendell got up on the bandstand with the bass, and I got up behind the drums … and in walked Duke Ellington, looking like a million bucks. He came up to tinkle on the piano, and nobody else was there.

I looked up at Wendell and asked, "Is it always like this?"

He said, "Oh, yes, don't you know what Duke says?"

"What does Duke say?"

"I'm too busy with my music to be a disciplinarian."

Five minutes later, Harry Carney, his closest right-hand man, might sit down at his saxophone, and then a few more guys would come in, and by 8:30, only half the band was there. By 9:00, an hour after the drop started, the band was there. We played, Duke schmoozed for the hour, and Wendell said, "It's always like this."

Now, when you worked with the Basie band, everybody would be in their chairs at ten to 8:00. Snooky Young worked with Basie, and he said it wasn't from fear; it was pride. I'm not sure why it wasn't the same with Ellington. He was genius, as far as I'm concerned, but his was the most loosely wrapped band. With Basie, it was different. I can tell you from working with Basie that without his saying a word, just looking at somebody, he put out a certain message: you don't want to screw up.

Duke's attitude, on the other hand, was "La di da, I'm too busy with my music." I've never known a band that could sound so far apart, one night from the other, as Duke's band. It could sound great one night and another night just okay, and I think it was that lack of discipline. For a genius like Duke, who accomplished so much with a band, I feel funny saying that, but I was witness to it.

I remember one time I was at a rehearsal of Duke's; I was just visiting, not playing. The manager said, "Okay, 12:00 noon rehearsal tomorrow." And

Cootie Williams, one of the trumpet players, said, "I'm not coming to no damn 12:00 noon rehearsal,"—just like that, out loud.

And I thought, "Wow, really? Is he not going to come to the rehearsal?" Nobody said anything to him. Maybe he didn't come to the damn 12:00 noon rehearsal. Maybe he came to the 1:00 damn rehearsal. I couldn't believe how blatant he was about it.

It was a wonderful experience working with Duke. I was scared to death part of the time, but after a while, I figured if they were going to put up with me, I was going to sit back and try to enjoy it.

BENNY GOODMAN

When I came back to New York after working with Charlie Ventura, I had a pretty good reputation. That kind of a jazz name, though, doesn't get you into the studios; it's a different world. I was back in New York, and the phone rang. It was Benny Goodman's manager, saying Benny Goodman would like me to go to Europe with him. That was a very big deal for me. We dickered and dockered, and we settled on a salary of $200 a week, which in 1950 wasn't bad. I signed a contract for the tour, which was three weeks. The other issue I negotiated was when they were fitting us for uniforms. They were white tuxedos: double-breasted coats with black slacks and tuxedo shirts. I said, "I have to have two jackets." The management was there and said, "What do you mean, two jackets?" And I said, "I'm not going unless I have two jackets, because I perspire a lot. If we're going to do a concert with a break in the middle, I want to have a dry jacket and a dry shirt to put on for the second half." I was very firm about it. I wouldn't have gone, either. It was that important to me. And I got it. They were nice jackets, too.

I always liked Benny Goodman, even though he was a strange person. I had always loved his playing, and he was going to have a band with Zoot Sims on tenor, Roy Eldridge on trumpet, Toots Thielemans on guitar, Dick Hyman on piano, and a very nice girl named Nancy Reed as a singer. He would pick up a very fine bass player named Charlie Small in England. I was surprised to find out that this was the first time he was going to Europe, unlike Louie Armstrong, who was a king in Europe during the '30s and '40s. Benny had never gone out of the country, even though he was the king of swing in the '30s. He was a strange cookie. He did great—he packed every place we went … Italy, Paris.

Before I went on tour with Benny Goodman, I visited Lionel Hampton. He used to let me sit in with his band in New York when he was there. After I played a little, he took me aside in the dressing room and said, "I hear you're going out with the old man. Here's how you get along with him. If you do what I tell you, you'll be cool. He will get weird on you, because he gets weird on everybody and especially on drummers. When he gets weird, acts weird, looks weird, you get weirder than him. That's what I used to do, and he never bothered me. He bothered a lot of other people who let him get to them."

When we were doing our first appearance in Paris, we had a sound check and rehearsal. I didn't know how to get a cab in Paris, so I was about half an hour late. By the time I got there, Benny was sitting on a chair by the stage door. He took his glasses off and looked at me like he was going to kill me. I remembered what Hamp had said, so I said—and I don't know where I got the guts to say it—"Benny, are we going to fuck around all day, or are we going to play?" He looked at me and must have thought, "I've got a crazy one here," but he said to everyone, "The kid's right. Let's play." He never bothered me after that. If it hadn't been for Lionel, I would have said, "Oh, Benny, I'm so sorry," and that would have been terrible. I had a pretty nice four weeks with him in Europe, even though he really had a reputation for being very bad on drummers.

Touring in Europe for the first time was interesting. In Italy, after we played, the audience would stomp and boo, and it was a little scary. The promoter came rushing out to the wings and said, "No, no, no, no. That means they love you." In other words, it was good if they made that booing sound, and they banged their feet on the floor, that was their super applause. We were relieved. I really thought there was going to be a riot because they hated us, but they loved us. We got about three encores in Rome. It was nice also that every once in a while in foreign countries, we'd see American musicians that we knew. I particularly was pleased to hang out for a while with Kenny Clarke. He was in Paris, teaching and playing. Many of the black musicians had a much freer time or better life in Europe or Scandinavia.

Benny Goodman was somewhat detached from reality and very self-absorbed. One story about him is that he wanted the singer Helen Forrest to come to his house to run down a few tunes. They were sitting in his living room, and she said, "It's kinda cold in here, Benny," and he said, "Oh, okay." He left the room and came back wearing a sweater. When Helen would tell this story, she would finish by saying, "Only Benny."

When Zoot Sims got too much applause in Norway, where they liked a little more of the modern approach, Benny took Zoot's solos away the next night. We had a seven-piece band. We needed to stretch the program by giving Roy Eldridge a solo, Zoot Sims a solo—everybody. I didn't have a drum solo, but I was okay with that. Benny was egomaniacal.

In Paris, Roy Eldridge played "After You're Gone," and he also sang the famous "Let Me Off Uptown." He tore the Parisian Opera House apart with those numbers ... and the next night he had no solos. That showed me that Benny was a truly egomaniacal person. He had Roy Eldridge, one of the world's greatest historical players, and he took it all away from him. Then, a few nights later, he eased up and gave Roy a solo but not in the same area. And when Zoot went to Scandinavia, he didn't give Zoot any more solos while we were there. Wacky, huh?

One of the reasons I always loved Duke Ellington is because when someone would say to him, "You write special pieces for your guys, and you show them off all the time," he'd say, "The better they do, the more it shines on me." I'm paraphrasing, but that's what he basically said. I think that's a wonderful attitude.

There's a story that is popularly known about Benny, and I believe it to be true. There was a wonderful girl named Joya Sherrill who sang with Duke. Many years later, she traveled with Benny on a tour. She bought a brand new camera, and when Benny saw it, he purportedly took the camera to look at it. Then someone said, "Hey, Benny," and instead of handing it back to Joya, he just dropped the camera on the ground and walked away. She burst into tears. I've heard that story from a few people. He lived in his own little world. When he passed away, I think there were three people at his service: Muriel, his long time secretary; his daughter; and his wife.

Still, he was great fun to play with, and I loved playing with him. I knew how to play for him. A lot of people said, "Gee, you got a be-bop name with Charlie Ventura, but how are you going to get along with Benny Goodman?" and I said, "You've got to be kidding. I'm not going to play for Benny Goodman the way I played with Charlie Ventura. Duh!" For Benny, I played swing style—simpler.

It was a lovely tour, although, not unexpectedly, he screwed us at the last minute. When we were in Paris, which was one of our first stops, we had a few days off after one of our concerts. Roy Eldridge got an offer to make a record for a French company, and so he took me; Charlie, the bass player; Zoot Sims; and Dick Hyman, the piano player, and we made the record. I think we all made about ten dollars. Benny later asked Roy what we did on our day off, and in all innocence, Roy told Benny that we'd made a record. Benny said, "That's nice," and didn't say another word. When it came time to get our last paycheck at the end of the tour, Muriel, his secretary, said, "Benny's not paying you for the last week. You broke the contract. His contract said 'exclusive services.'" We all said, "But we had a couple of days off with nothing to do." Then we found out that he had gone to Monte Carlo and supposedly had lost $40,000 a few days before, so he was going to not pay the band that last week. Of course, none of us had any money left. Zoot Sims and I both got on the plane with two dollars between us. When we landed at Kennedy Airport, we got into a cab and went to Charlie's Tavern, which was the hangout for musicians in New York in Midtown. We went to Charlie and borrowed the cab money from him. That was the way Benny ended the tour. So when he called me a few months later to work, I told his manager, "I get paid in cash before the job; otherwise, I don't play for Benny Goodman." And that's the way I played some jobs for him. The manager would come up and give me the cash before I played. I only played with him a few times after that, but I only did it on my terms.

Benny was known to be a cheapskate. When you took a cab with him, you wanted to be the first one out, or you would be stuck paying the fare. I was in an Italian restaurant, sitting with some of the band guys, and Benny was at another table. When he got his bill, he autographed it, got up, and was starting to walk out when the owner (or the chef) came after him with a big knife. Benny thought autographing the bill would take care of it—but he then paid the bill, believe me. Oh, he was a cheapskate.

One time he tried to sell me some cymbals that an Italian guy had given him, and he asked me what I'd give him for the cymbals. I said to him, "Didn't he give those to you to give to me?"

He said, "No, he gave them to me, but I thought if you liked them, you'd give me some money for them."

I hit one or two of them, and they sounded like something that should be around a cow's neck. I said, "No, Benny, these cymbals are just right for you," and I walked away.

I had to learn to stand up for myself; I was infamous for not taking crap from people. Yet I was easy to work with. I always felt if someone insulted my integrity and didn't give me respect, I wouldn't care if I lost the job. I would speak my mind. I felt that keeping my self-respect and integrity was more important than anything. And really, that never happened. Some people like to have the upper hand, but at the same time, if you deal with them, there's something in them that then respects you.

One time I was sitting with a thirty-piece orchestra at Columbia Records at the famous Columbia Studio, 30th Street, in New York City, and we started playing this poppy date with Ray Conniff, who sold millions of records. Mitch Miller was producing, and he stopped the record, saying, "Shaughnessy, I'm not happy."

I said, "Oh, okay, what's going on?"

Mitch said, "The feel of this thing is not the right feel for this song."

"It's the first time we've played it down," I told him. "I got quarter notes on the music."

"I'd like to have that nice, buoyant shuffle, like on that hit record I made, 'Baubles, Bangles, and Beads,'" Mitch said. "Did you ever hear that?"

I said I had.

He said, "Do you think maybe you could approximate that?"

"I'll tell you what," I said. "I guarantee it, because I made that record with you." And of course the whole band fell apart.

Mitch waited a minute and said, "Okay, then, I guess you'll get it."

POST-BENNY GOODMAN

I worked a few times, a couple of weeks each time, with Lucky Millinder at the Savoy Ballroom, and that was very important to me because that band had a rhythm-and-blues groove and feel. It was eighteen pieces, and I followed the stupendous Art Blakey—good luck! Let's put it this way: like every other job I did, I did the best I could. The guys were quite nice to me, and I thought I had good feel—it helped to work with a big rhythm-and-blues band. I hate to always use the racial terms of white band and black band, but some of the black bands that were very rhythm-and-blues–oriented definitely had a different feel. They just did—like Benny Goodman had his own type of swing. It didn't have a very bluesy-based swing. It was great, but it was different, and so I played differently.

MAKING LEMONADE OUT OF LEMONS– THE CHITLIN' CIRCUIT

So here I was, having worked with Charlie Ventura when he was hot, just making medium money—it might have been $150 or $200. I made $200 per week with Benny Goodman in Europe. That wasn't big money, but it was pretty good at the time. But when I worked with Charlie, we didn't stay in fancy hotels. We stayed in a lot of motels, and we shared rooms. I roomed with Benny Green, the great trombone player, who was a wonderful guy, and we had a lot of fun. I roomed with Roy Eldridge when I was with Benny Goodman, and he was a lot of fun too. We lugged a five-gallon jug of wine up to our room in Rome, because we couldn't brush our teeth with the water—it was spoiled—so we brushed our teeth and washed ourselves with wine. With Charlie, a hot act, we didn't stay at any place you'd write home about.

When I went out with Lucky Millinder in about 1951, we played on the "Chitlin' Circuit"—the Apollo in New York, the Royal in Baltimore, the Howard in Washington, and the Earl in Philadelphia—which primarily played to the black audience, although there were white fans. (I saw Buddy Rich play at the Apollo when his arm was in a sling, and he played with one arm.) The guys were great to me, no racial draft at all. I was the only white guy in the band at that particular time, and the only thing said to me by some of the older guys in the band was, "Eddie, when we're riding on the bus, and we're going through big cities, stay down low and keep a cap on your head. Once in a while, you'll hit some of these real redneck sheriffs, and if they see a white boy on a black bus, they might want to take you off and work you up a little bit."

So on the Chitlin' Circuit, the bus would stop at a nice-looking, respectable brownstone house, and they'd drop off four, five, or six guys, and then we'd go to another house, and they'd drop off four or five guys. The deal was that for years on the black circuit of show business, they had all these homes that regularly acted as hotels for the guys on the road. They were extremely cheap. I think I paid two dollars a night. I had my own room, with clean sheets and blankets, and for a dollar, I got a supper of all I could eat. Now, this beat the hell out of what I'd had before, even when I was with a hot act. They had learned how to live in a good, decent manner, while prejudice had kept them from staying in the white hotels and restaurants. In a way, they were actually doing better than the white groups. I did better with Lucky's band on the Chitlin' Circuit than I had before with a couple of other bands, including Charlie Ventura. I can remember how Mona Hinton, one of my favorite people in the world, and her hubby, Milt Hinton, had their own Pullman cars when traveling in the Calloway band. Mona would go to the black neighborhood, knock on a few doors, and ask if she could use their kitchen, and would a few ladies help? She would bring in six or eight chickens, vegetables, and such, and the black people were so thrilled that it was Cab Calloway's band that they were standing in line to help. Mona said they would all eat in the home, bypassing all the redneck stuff and prejudice. I couldn't get over how the black musicians had surmounted this. They had made lemonade out of lemons.

It was early morning, and we were playing in Maryland with a dance act. This guy Tony came out; he was going to tap dance. Okay, go play Tony's music. We got to a place in the music called "stop time," where the band stops, but the tap dancer does some good stuff. This guy's time with his feet was all over the place. It was up to me to bring the band back in properly, and I was tapping my foot, thinking the hell with him. This went on for two choruses of stop time, and it was maddening. He wasn't near the time. I came off the bandstand after rehearsing this act, and Lucky Millinder, who was a short, stocky, good-looking, ebullient man with a great head of hair, came rushing up to me and said, "Hey, Shaun, no, we all don't got it." He couldn't wait to say that to me. We laughed about that for a couple of years.

Lucky didn't read music, but he really knew how to organize an arrangement. If B should be at C and D at E, he knew that. He knew that if there were too many solos in the arrangement, we should take one or two out. He had a little tambourine, and he would stand in front of the band and hit it—and it was very infectious. The people loved it. The dancers at the Savoy loved it. He was a good leader.

A person doesn't have to be the most technically trained. It was often said of Chick Webb that he didn't have to look at a piece of music—he couldn't read music—yet he always could change an arrangement around.

By the way, I saw Chick Webb play live for a mini-second. Someone sent me a clip from a documentary about Chick Webb at the Savoy Ballroom. Don't forget: my drums sat in the same place as Chick Webb's did, which thrilled me to no end. I had never seen anything with Chick moving, except on that clip. He had an incredible ease that I could see in those three seconds.

Anyway, Lucky was a very good bandleader. He would say funny things to me like, "There's an eight-bar drum break in this new arrangement we're playing. White boy, you'd better keep 'em dancing." I'd play very simple.

I enjoyed playing at the Savoy, not just for the history of it, although the history was terrific, but because I really enjoyed the experience. One of my funniest experiences was one New Year's Eve. I came off the bandstand really perspiring. A guy in a green suit came up to me and asked my name. "My name is Ed Shaughnessy," I told him.

"Well, damn, you can play them drums," he said.

"Thank you very much," I said. "What's your name?"

"My name is Bill Owens, and I'm from Cinci-fuckin'-atti."

I said kiddingly back, "Bill Owens, from Cinci-fuckin'- atti, I'm really happy to meet you," and he bought me a beer.

I worked with Lucky probably two different times at the Savoy. When we played the Savoy, we played a week or two, and I think I did two two-week stints. And there was another band on another bandstand, so when we weren't playing, the music never stopped. One of the best bands was Buddy Johnson, who had a wonderful singer, ala Billy Eckstine, named Arthur Prysock. Arthur was quite famous in that romantic singing circle of the '40s and '50s.

MINGUS, JOCKEYS, AND CLAMS— OH, MY!

Charlie Mingus was a force of nature and a great guy to work with. He had a mercurial temperament, but I never got on the bad side of him. He hit a few people, put his hand through a wall, and jumped up and down on a bass when going down to one of the clubs because the owner wouldn't pay him his money.

Some people say that Buddy Rich, a man famous for his temper, is only the man he appears to be on the tapes they've heard where he's yelling at his band, but that isn't accurate. And just like Buddy Rich, Mingus had a lot of other sides. I enjoyed working with Charlie. He would say things like, "Shlop it up, shlop it up," meaning, get a more sloppy feel, but this was good musical criticism. He wasn't saying I was a horse's ass or that I couldn't play; he was saying, this is a bluesy shlop. And I would say, "Okay, Mingus," because he was right. A lot of people would say that they would get educated with Mingus, even if it hurt, because he would tell people things that were right, even though sometimes it was a little hard to take. He was not tactful. I honestly think he was one of the most talented people in jazz ever, not only because he was a brilliant virtuoso bass player but because of how he wrote music.

He and I lived not far from each other in Queens when I was married the first time, and he came to the door one night without calling. Usually, he would call, but this time he didn't. And he said, "Eddie, take a ride with me."

Somebody from my wife's family was over, so I said, "Mingus, I can't. I have company. We're going to eat."

"Come take a ride with me," he said again.

"Mingus, I can't. And please, call the next time, like you usually do."

"Okay, man," he said. "I'm sorry you can't come with me." The next day in the local paper, I read that someone had gone around with a big bucket of white paint and a brush and had painted all the black lawn jockeys in Queens. Of course, that's what Mingus had wanted me to do with him that night. I asked him later, "That was you, wasn't it?" And he said, "Oh, yeah, man. I get sick and tired of those damn jockeys."

Here's another story about Mingus that's worth telling: He once said, "I'd love to get some clams. There's a place down on the waterfront. My car is laid up, so would you take me for some clams tomorrow?" We were working at the Half Note. He had a very fine drummer named Dannie Richmond, but Dannie had a few health problems, so when he was under the weather, I would work with Mingus. Mingus had different phases. He had his Oriental phase, when he wore a big pigtail and an Oriental gown, but at this time, he was in his English phase. So when I picked him up, he was wearing a three-piece black suit, with a matching shirt and tie, and a Hamburg derby, and he was carrying a cane. He looked very classy.

As we drove down to the waterfront, where all the stevedores hung out, I thought to myself, "I wonder how it's going to go over when he walks into the clam place. That's kind of a rough-and-ready crowd." But I certainly wasn't going to say anything to Mingus. I parked my car, and we walked into the place, which had sawdust all over the floor. A lot of those tough-looking guys looked up, but Mingus projected something that said, "You wouldn't want to fuck with me," and nobody looked twice. He didn't have to do anything; it was just something subtle that he projected. He had four helpings of clams and some oysters and insisted on paying for it, and we didn't have a bit of trouble.

But you need to know that he was a great guy. I even hired him once to play with Flip Phillips, who was a very good jazz saxophone player but tended to play a little for the crowd. We needed a bass player out on Long Island, because the bass player Flip hired bowed out, and Flip said, "You gotta get me somebody."

I said, "I could get you Charlie Mingus. I know he's not working."

"Charlie Mingus?" Flip asked. "Will he play for me?"

I said sure, and then I called up Mingus and said, "Hey, Mingus, come on—you wanna work Saturday night? I'll pick you up and take you home."

"Sure, sure," he said. "Who we playing for?"

"Flip Phillips." "I've heard of him," Mingus said. "Okay." And he was like a dream all night, playing standards. And if Flip did a little for the crowd, Mingus would go, "Yeah, Flip!"

Later, Flip said, "Boy, I never would have guessed! He was such fun." We all had a good time.

TOMMY DORSEY

I got a call from Tommy Dorsey. I think Louie Bellson recommended me. I worked with Tommy in New York at a theater for a couple of weeks.

I liked working with him. He was tough, though. Everything had better be right, all the time, but I think that's the way it should be anyway. I used to play Charlie Parker records one floor above Tommy's dressing room at the Capital Theater, and he'd come out and yell, "Turn that shit off!" And I'd yell back, "Maybe if you'd listen, you'd learn something." I swear, may God be my judge, that's what I'd say. And Sid, the guy in sax section, said, "Eddie, you just killed your job." But instead, Tommy went back in his room, laughing. He thought it was hysterical. I also played Yma Sumac records, a Peruvian singer who was very popular in the '50s. She sang very high in perfect pitch, word-less, but higher than the dogs could hear. It drove Tommy crazy.

A CLOSE CALL

One night I was running late to the Dorsey gig at the Capital Theater because we were having drinks over at the bar on 8th Avenue. The stage was literally starting to go up as I arrived. I opened the door, stopped the stage, and crawled up onto it– I had about one and a half feet to squeeze my body in. Tommy said later if the stage had started again, it would have cut me right in half. I won't repeat the things he said to me that night. I managed to get up on the stage, run up on the drums, and by the time the lights came up, I was there. It was really foolish, but I didn't want to not be on stage when the lights went up. I didn't do things like that very often. That told me a drink at lunchtime might not be a good idea.

We did an album called *The Most Beautiful Girl in the World*, which was a nice album and did pretty well for Tommy for those days. He offered me a three-year contract and said, "I did it for Buddy Rich, I did it for Louie Bellson, and I'll do it for you." At that time, however, my mother was sick, so I said, "Tommy, I gotta stay around in case I'm needed by my mom. I can't really go out on the road."

He was pretty gruff and said, "Well, kid, you'll be sorry at some later day."

And I said, "Yeah, I know, Tommy, but family is family—you know that."

"Yeah, I suppose so," he told me, "but you're making a big mistake. You're making a big mistake."

His band went out on the road, and I felt pretty bad that I was missing a big opportunity. Even then, he had a high profile, and he featured his drum-mer. I didn't know what I was going to do; I really didn't have any work. And then the phone rang. It was a guy named Lou Shoobe, the contractor from CBS, and he said, "I saw the last show you did with Tommy Dorsey last week. You can read great."

I said, "I can read fly shit."   "You played for a juggling act, a dance act, for a singer, and the band music," he said, "and you did all of those things extremely well. I've got Steve Allen from California, and we're going to put him on the air five days a week. He wants a jazz band. He doesn't want studio guys who aren't jazzers. How would you like to have that job?"

I felt so lucky. It's okay to say I had the goods, but Lou Shoobe was in the audience for the last show I did with Tommy Dorsey. That's why I always say a little bit of the good luck is necessary, even if you've got the goods.

CBS—1956

I went to work on a five-day-a-week show with Steve Allen, and it was very good money at that time, compared to band money—something like $300 a week, and it was easy work, a couple of hours a day, playing with a little jazz group. It didn't last too long, because Steve Allen wasn't really right for day-time. He was too hip. He was a really eclectic man. He wrote about a thousand songs, and he was very intelligent. Once he hit nighttime, that was his thing. But I had that job for six months and got my foot in the door, as I was on CBS staff. I did a few other little shows, and in the meantime, I was working in jazz clubs at night, which was really the music I loved, so I felt very fortunate. Jazz clubs, at the most, paid $70 to $90 a week.

FIRST MARRIAGE

I met a very attractive gal, five years older than me, and we got married when I was 22, which was around 1951—I was young and naïve. We stayed married for about eight years, although after about five years, I knew it wasn't very good. I was so green and really didn't know the right kind of gal for me. I should not have gotten married; I should have just been a musician for another ten years. She was a funny girl. She wished to be a star, like many people, without being of star material. She admired what I did and how successful I was at it, but at the same time she resented it a little bit. And she was the kind of gal who, when I got the offer to go play with Benny Goodman for President Kennedy, said, "Why can't I go?" I had to say, "Honey, I had to be cleared by the FBI six months ago, and we can't take people with us." Nobody, including Mrs. Goodman, went along—it was just the band, and that was the deal. They didn't want to have to clear other people. That was in '61 or '62.

The band that night was Teddy Wilson on piano, George Duvivier on bass, Benny, and me on drums. We played at the White House Correspondents Dinner, and it was a thrill to shake President Kennedy's hand. He really liked jazz, and he told us how much he liked the group. Peter Sellers was the opening act, and I saw that man sweating backstage—you would think he had never performed before. I said, "Mr. Sellers, what a pleasure. Everybody is so happy you're here." He was beside himself. He said, "Oh, my God, I hope it goes okay, oh my God …" And then he went out and killed 'em with a bunch of funny impressions.

Did you know that Jack Benny used to throw up before shows? Rochester often brought him the pail. That's a well-known fact. My wife knows that firsthand, because she was working in radio at the time. Nerves. Then Jack would go out and kill the audience.

After getting a divorce, I tried to keep my ex-wife happy. Financially, I pretty much gave her everything I had—that way, I didn't have alimony to worry about, like all my friends. We were friendly after that. She'd come sweeping into the Tonight Show in California, all dolled up. "Hi, baby, how are you?" I'd greet her. The guys would ask, "Who's that?" And I'd say, "That's my ex-wife." And they'd respond, "Wow!" I'm glad we were on good terms. I've always thought it's the saddest thing when people who have lived together and shared a lot of their lives end up being very bitter with each other.

JOE BUSHKIN

Joe Bushkin was a force of nature. He was a small, slight, dapper, wiry man who had become somewhat famous with Tommy Dorsey. He also wrote a thing called "I Love a Piano." He was a good jazz pianist, and he got this gig at the Ember's three or four times a year. The key to why he was there wasn't just that he played great; it was because he was married to a society wife, and she brought all the big muckety-muck money people like Tallulah Bankhead into the club. I'd hear Tallulah's voice say to him, "Oh, Joey dear."

Working with Joe was just fun. When I'd come to work, he would say, "How do you feel? I can get you up, or I can take you down or leave you where you are," meaning he had different and various medications. I used to say, "I'm pretty cool, Joe." And he'd say, "That's fine; just so you know."

He himself was on the ball, although he rushed like crazy. He took me aside and said, "Jo Jones really bawled me out the other night and said, 'Boy, you're really rushing more than you're usually rushing.' Do you think I rush?" I said, "I'll tell you what I think: it's your band." He said, "That's a good answer," and he laughed. Of course he rushed. I had a lot of fun with him. He had a lovely wife named Fran, who looked somewhat like Tallulah, with the hair over one eye. That was the era of the black dresses and minks and diamonds—that was the way those gals used to come in. It was a certain look, the money look. In those days, there was no faux fur. Three or four gals would be sitting at the same table wearing black dresses, with lots of diamonds, and the mink coat over the back of the chair.

In earlier years, women never went out without a hat and gloves. Ilene told me she once went up to her agent's office to pick up a check on a Saturday, and she was wearing jeans, a sweatshirt, and a jacket. He came down on her, saying, "What are you doing, going out on the street like that?"

She said, "It's the weekend. I'm relaxing."

"If you look like a million dollars, you make a million dollars," he told her. "Don't ever come to this office like that again." And she said she never did. She came fully dressed, with heels and gloves.

MID FIFTIES AND GARRY MOORE

I got the offer to work on Garry Moore's show. I figured it was a morning show, so I could play all the jazz clubs at night. The work I did at CBS for those four years never interfered with my jazz playing at night. It was daytime work. They hired me because I'd come in to do a sub thing. They only had guitar, bass, piano, and clarinet, and Garry, the boss, liked the way it sounded with my drumming. That was where I first met Ilene—I was married at the time; she was divorced. She was doing two weeks on that show as a sub.

The musicians were all well known-people: Carl Kress was a historic guitar player, Ernie Caceres was on clarinet, Trigger Alpert was a well-known and wonderful bassist who had gained fame with the Glenn Miller Band, and Howard Smith was the leader who wrote great little arrangements, played very well, and had become well known with Tommy Dorsey. They were like typical New York studio guys, most of whom had a good jazz background. That was a pleasant, nice job, but it ended because they offered Garry a nighttime slot, which never went well for him; he admitted later that he should have stayed where he was.

I didn't go with him when he went to nighttime—that was a whole different package with different people. I started doing a few freelance CBS things. I wasn't a very happy camper, though, and I gave my notice. A lot of people asked me how I could give my notice when I was making between $350 and $400 a week—this was in the mid-1950s. But one day, a big, chunky guy who played baritone sax came up to me and said, "Why do you always try to play your best up here?"

"Excuse me?" I responded.

"I notice no matter what type of show we're doing," he said, "you always try to play your best."

And I said, "That's what we're supposed to do."

He shook his head. "Nobody cares up here," he told me. This was a guy who kept a golf bag next to him so he could run right out of the studio to the golf course.

I went to the contractor's office later that day and turned in my notice. I said, "This is not the place for me." Besides, Teddy Charles and I were thinking of starting a little quartet to play jazz clubs, so there were other fish to fry.

THE COMPOSER'S WORKSHOP

I was asked to join a very democratic group with Charles Mingus, Teddy Charles, Teo Macero, and Eddie Bert (a great trombone player), and a few other musicians. It was an eight-piece, sometimes ten-piece band. The idea was to encourage composers to write new and different music that stretched the boundaries for it. We considered it a completely democratic group, and we put on a couple of concerts. We would split whatever small amount of money was made. If we could pay for the hall and play the music, that's all it was about.

The premise was very altruistic and all about the music. We did have some very interesting and unusual music written for us by Mingus and Teddy Charles and Teo Macero. They really stretched the boundaries.

THE GREAT VOCALISTS I WORKED WITH

Billie Holiday   I got a call from Columbia Records some time in 1954, asking me to record with Billie Holiday for an album called *A Recital by Billie Holiday* on Clef Records. I was knocked out. I didn't know Billie Holiday, but I used to go see her on 52nd Street when I was young. They said, "You might be interested to know it's Oscar Peterson, Ray Brown, Charlie Shavers on trumpet, and you."

I was only about twenty-three years old, and I said to myself, "Gee, with Don Lamond and all the great drummers in New York, I wonder why they called me?" And then I thought, "Well, because I can play very good brushes, and I can play very fast," which is what Ray Brown and Oscar Peterson knew about me—they were going to do "What a Little Moonlight Can Do," which is very fast. I even wondered why when they called me for Basie, ten years later, because New York was loaded with supreme drummers, but a couple of guys in the Basie band had worked with me.

I was thrilled to death. It was a very prestigious call, and I was really excited. I idolized Oscar Peterson and Ray Brown. Billie was in good shape, and she was very warm and welcoming. When I left, I had wings on my feet. They were all so nice to me. I had played with a lot of famous people by then, including Charlie Parker, but I have to say, Oscar Peterson and Ray Brown are such dynamic rhythm players. In fact, I once heard the two of them follow Maynard Ferguson's band at Carnegie Hall, and I think they swung harder than Ferguson's whole band—and it was a good band. But they just had that thing. Billie was singing really well at that time, and it was such a great honor for me. She was definitely an iconic singer. Everything back then was cut live, of course, and it was like we were in a nightclub with the earphones on.

Ella Fitzgerald   I had a chance to work for two weeks with Ella Fitzgerald at a very nice hotel called the America in New York—it doesn't exist anymore, but at the time it was on 50-something Street and Broadway. This was in the '60s. The great pianist Tommy Flanagan, whom we lost in 2001, called me and said, "I know you're doing the Tonight Show, but could you do Ella?"

And I said, "You gotta be kidding! I'll take off the *Tonight Show*."

He said, "You don't have to. We don't start until 9:00."

I was getting off at 6:30 from the Tonight Show at the time. I took one day off for a rehearsal.

From the minute I saw that woman, it was magic. She came up and put her arms around me and said, "You've made me so happy by playing with us."

I said, "Are you kidding? I'd play for nothing." She was so welcoming. When a legendary person is like that, it makes you play even better. She just made me feel so good. Playing with her was like working with a great improvisational horn player or pianist. She never did it exactly the same way twice. There is an album out now of her singing at a Los Angeles club—she's in the rarest form, talking, kidding. It's some of the best Ella I've heard, and I've heard a lot of good Ella—I loved her live.

Ella gave me a pair of solid gold cufflinks—I just looked at them the other day—thanking me for playing with her. I said, "Oh, please, I should be buying you some jewelry." Sweet lady. She sure could swing.

Peggy Lee   I spent a lot of very pleasant nights and weeks, working with Peggy Lee in the '50s and a little in the '60s. She came to New York and appeared in a club called La Vien Rose for an entire month. She packed the house every single night, standing room only. We had a wonderful group with Jimmy Rowles on piano, Joe Mondragan on bass, and Pete Condoli on trumpet from California. And then Peggy used me because I had made her famous record "Lover."

I had a wonderful time with her. Peggy was a unique person. She was very spiritual, and she felt if you didn't give a hug and a kiss before every show, it wouldn't be a good show, so that's something we had to do—not that it was unpleasant, but she was funny that way.

Some people thought of her as kind of spacey, in a way, but she wasn't really, when it came down to the music or her presentation. Boy, you could hear a pin drop in the room when she sang a soft ballad. It was remarkable to me. Other than her voice, there wasn't a sound. She was one of the great storytellers of all time and a kind lady. I also worked the Copacabana with her. She would have a big suite upstairs and tell the guys, "My suite is your suite. Come up to the suite. I have food; I have drinks." Whenever I worked with Peggy, it was like family, and that was something very special. Ella was the same way; she would want us to come in the room and would ask, "Would you like a beer? Would you like a Coke?" The biggest stars of all are usually great. It's those pretenders you have to look out for.

Carmen McRae   I made one album with Carmen. I got to know her a little bit because she was married to Kenny Clarke, the drummer, and sometimes when I was working on Carmen's album, he would tell me, "Say hello to Carmen for me," and so I'd pass along that message. I didn't do a lot of live playing with her. I loved her because she could go over to the piano if the pianist was not playing something quite right, and she'd sit down and play it the right way. She started her career like Sarah Vaughan—both of them played piano. They accompanied themselves until they got big enough to hire someone to play for them.

She was very musical, with a wry sense of humor. If somebody made a mistake, she'd say, "Hey, Joe, do you think we ought to try this one again?" She'd never say, "You played a bad note." I loved her.

Billy Eckstine I never made a record with Billy, but I worked with him in clubs, mostly at the Royal Roost in New York, where they had Charlie Parker's band, Charlie Ventura's band, and Billy Eckstine—an all-star billing. We stayed for two months because the business was so good. Billy Eckstine, whom I already knew, said, "Could I ask you a favor? It's an awfully big favor. I've got this little trio, but would you play conga drum with me? Don't worry; I'll pay you. I just love the conga drum sound when I'm singing."

I said, "Sure, Billy, I'll do it as a favor." He was a nice, sweet man, and I thought that instead of sitting on my ass, eating coffee cake next door, I'd play—and I could still be off during Charlie Parker's set. Billy Eckstine was a lovely man and had a vibrato you could drive a truck through. I loved it.

Tony Bennett Tony Bennett really endeared himself to me when he stuck up for me one time when we were making a record at Columbia Records. The producer stopped the record and said over the mike, "I don't think Shaughnessy is bopping enough." Now, this was behind Tony Bennett.

Tony says over the mike, "What do you mean, bopping enough?" The producer said, "He should bop more, make more accents and things." And Tony said, "I have Ed here because he has good taste. I like what he's doing; that's why I have him come here. Is that okay with you?" The guy never said another word. Why would I bop in back of Tony Bennett? Knowing what not to do is just as important as knowing what to do. Later, I thanked Tony, and he said, "That guy's an ass. What does he think? You should be bopping behind my vocal?" It was an album that did very well for Tony.

Barbra Streisand   This particular incident deserves an honorable mention. Sometime around 1958 or 1959 I was working in a small Greenwich Village nightclub, which name escapes me, in New York City. They were having a singing contest over a two-week period on the weekends. On the second weekend, this kid came in to sing. She was probably about 16 or 17, all dressed in black, a turtleneck and pants tucked into high boots, not a touch of make-up. It was certainly not close to a nightclub singer's usual look. Most girls wore long gowns with fancy hair-do's and tons of make-up. Her hair was simply pulled back in a pony tail with a black ribbon. And then...my God...she started to sing "Stardust" and I almost dropped my brushes! The sound that came out of the young Barbra Streisand throat was unbelievably beautiful and she told a story. I had already worked with some famous singers but this girl was something else. Needless to say, she won the contest and I went home to my wife saying, 'I played for the next superstar of show-biz! You have to hear her to believe her!' It was a real kick to see Babs soon on Broadway in I Can Get It For You Wholesale and all the multitude of triumphs...but what a special thrill to be there at the start! A real privilege.

DRUMMERS I WOULD LIKE TO MENTION– THE OLD GUARD

Big Sid Catlett   When I was fifteen years old and in high school, I went to 52nd Street, snuck into the club, and ordered a Coke. Eventually, Big Sid Catlett saw me, asked me if I was a drummer, and let me play a few times. He was very good to me and friendly, and he encouraged me to work on my reading, so I could play shows when I didn't have jazz work. He moved with the grace of a ballet dancer. He was about six foot three and looked like he should have been a New York Giants linebacker, and yet he played with a delicacy that was amazing. Some people say I'm graceful when I play, and I think it has to do with the fact that he was my first impression of a pro drummer. That was the way he moved.

Among the great brush players I heard were Jo Jones with Count Basie, Shelly Manne, Kenny Clarke, Denzel Best, but my favorite of all was the eminent Sid Catlett. I thought Sidney had a great little snap to his brush playing. It made you tap your foot. He'd start a lot of tunes with his quartet by playing a brush intro, just playing rhythm, and he'd get you jumping right away, before the band even started. It's like trying to pick between different kinds of food—they're all good. There were a lot of really fine brush players back in those days, particularly in the swing era and coming out of the swing era.

Max Roach   Max Roach was an extremely good brush player also. He was able to manipulate the brushes at those up-tempo speeds that they played with. I once caught him when he was playing with the Bud Powell Trio, and he was mad because Bud didn't let him play with sticks, just with brushes the whole time. Once in a while he would put his head down and play with the sticks just to do it, but most of the time Bud would only let him play with brushes.

Max was particularly friendly to me. He asked me to come up to his apartment, and he would show me how he practiced, his combinations. He had one of those quiet practice drum sets, not a real drum kit, because he lived in a New York apartment. He was very melodic—that was the key thing about him that was different—so he showed me how he practiced melodic things on the four-piece drum set. He'd play them, then reverse them, then inside out, and then outside in.

I said, "Oh, I see where you get some of that great freedom you have melodically."

He said, "Eddie, it's just like anything else on any other instrument. You just have to work them out, and then turn them inside out, then turn them around." I thought it was very interesting—Max was a very interesting man and had great logic to the way he practiced and developed his style. I think it's great that he became a professor at the University of Massachusetts, because I think he was gifted as a teacher as well. He showed me how he was constantly developing his melodic prowess on the drum set, as opposed to a technical guy who'd say, "Look at my left hand." There was none of that at all. It was all the entire instrument, making statements, which is quite a different approach from the technical guy who says something like, "Look at how fast my foot is."

One time, after he showed me all this, he said, "I want you to do me a favor, will you? I have to work this weekend, and Abbey has to attend a big affair." He was married to the singer Abbey Lincoln at the time. "I don't want her to go by herself. Would you escort her?" It was for some kind of Afro-American organization that Max was active in.

I said, "Sure."

Abbey had just had her hair cut in a style that was close to shaved—she called it a "nappy look"—and this was in the 1950s, way before anyone was doing this. As we walked into the ballroom, she said to me, "Watch everybody look at me, Ed, because they don't like it." She made the appearance for Max, and then we left.

It was really nice that he'd asked me to do this for him. And it was quite different from a year or two earlier when he came into Birdland. I had finished a rather hot set with Terry Gibbs. As I came off the stage, Max said, "What's the matter? Are the drums broke?"

And I said, "What?"

"What's the matter? Are the drums broke?" he repeated.

"No, Max, why?"

He said, "I just wondered," and he walked away. Art Blakey said to

43

me later, "You sounded too good. That's what guys say when you sound too good."

But a couple of years later, I became a friend of Max's, and he invited me to one or two record dates where he was doing some very futuristic, odd times in 7/4 and things like that, even before Dave Brubeck did "Take 5." All due credit to Dave Brubeck, but Max was a real forerunner of odd times, playing 7/4 upstairs with the hands, which is what the group and the jazz and everything was in, but keeping the 2/4 on the bottom—boom chick, boom chick, boom chick, which turned around to chick boom, chick boom, chick boom every two bars.

My reaction was "Oh, my God," because I had never heard anybody think of that or do that. It was one of those albums Max did during the civil rights upheaval, and he did "We Protest" and "The Freedom Now Suite." This piece was one of those pieces.

But I was the new gun in town when he made that comment about the drums being "broke." I had just come off of Charlie Ventura's band, with great big publicity, placing high in the polls out of nowhere, and now I was in New York, working in the jazz clubs. I was the competition. But after that one time, it was fine, and it turned around to the point where he asked me to escort his wife to an event. And more than once after that, he told me how good I sounded.

Art Blakey   Art was great because he was known to be "color blind." Coming from the background of being a coal miner's son, he didn't care if you were white, green, yellow, or purple, as long as you could play good. He would hire a Japanese musician or anyone from Mars.

One time I came off the stage when I was playing at Birdland, and there were a couple of black guys sitting at a table. One of them said, "Huh? What was that?" as I walked by. Blakey was walking down the aisle because he was the next act up, and he heard it. He took me aside and said, "If you weren't swinging your ass off, they wouldn't have said anything. Do you hear where I'm coming from? I heard you. I heard you." He was great that way. I always admired him because he was always like that, particularly in the '60s when a lot of racial attitudes were changing, and people like Oliver Nelson got criticized for using me and Phil Woods. Blakey wouldn't have any of it.

When I worked with Art Blakey, we used to say, "The laundry's in town." In the back of Birdland, up on a steam pipe, Art would have four shirts, and I'd have four shirts—eight shirts because we each played four sets at Birdland, and we both perspired a lot.

We worked hard there, from 9:30 p.m. to 3:00 a.m. That's why, when people would ask how I could sit and play those fast tempos, I'd say, "When you're playing like this over four or five sets a night, it becomes just like someone asking, 'How do you ice skate?'" Well, I did it a lot. That's what we did, and that's the best training I could have gotten. When we did a week or two at Birdland, it was like going to the gymnasium.

Although he wasn't a drummer, I'd also like to mention Horace Silver, the great pianist and bandleader, because he and I were part of that house rhythm section at Birdland, where we would play with different horn players. Horace was a remarkable player to play with. Almost every day, if I went to get a cymbal for a date of something, Horace was at the piano, practicing. I always admired him for that.

Gene Krupa   I only had the pleasure of meeting Gene two times, and he was the greatest gentleman you would ever want to meet. He was always so kind. He was a very classy man. He was known as a wild man on the drums, but in person he was a rather refined, classy guy. I thought that was great. I have a picture that I treasure that reads "To my favorite drummer," and I don't care if he gave that same picture to a thousand people. I think he liked me, though, because at the time, Charlie Ventura was the saxophone star of his band, and when Charlie left—with Gene's blessing—and started his own band, I was Charlie's drummer, so there was a little personal connection there. What a nice, kind man.

Jo Jones   When you're young and eager to learn and listen to jazz, like Kenny and I were, you figure out a lot of byways and highways. We found out there was a street entrance to the lower level of the Hotel Lincoln that was down at 34th Street and Broadway, which was the level that the Count Basie Band played on at the hotel. It was one story down from the street. This was a back entrance through that level—it actually was a stairway that went right down to the stage. So even though we couldn't see anything, if we snuck in that door, which was always open, and sat on the stairs, we could hear the Basie band live, really well. I mean, it was like we had a seat in the room where they were playing.

At least once a week, Kenny and I would go over to the Lincoln and sneak in the door—no one ever bothered us, ever. We were so lucky. We would sit there and listen to one or two sets of the Count Basie Band, and it was just remarkable, because I had never heard that band in person before. After we did that a couple of times, Kenny and I went out to the Adams Theater in New York by bus. The Adams Theater had a lot of great bands, particularly a lot of great black bands that you might not get to see as much in the middle of Manhattan. They would have Earl Hines and a few of the other fine black bands. When we went out there to see Basie, it was the first time I saw Jo Jones. I had heard him on record and at the Lincoln Hotel, but I had never seen him, and of course, the way he played was as mesmerizing in its own way as a Buddy Rich, or a Kenny Clarke, or a Max Roach, or any of the other great iconic figures. He had such an elegance and grandeur with the way he played the drums, it made me feel like this was the most elegant thing a man could do.

He had a great, wide-open musical sound, and he played a wonderful solo on the tune they called "Brushes." He played first with brushes, and then he put the brushes down, and for me it was a revelation when he played some solos with his bare hands and fingers. That's something I adapted from that day on—I certainly admit that I got that from Jo Jones. You get such a different sound when you play the drums with bare hands. Of course, I added some original stuff of my own, like singing Indian rhythms and then playing those back with the bare hands, like the tabla players did.

But there was Jo Jones, with the sweeping motion of the arms, which is the best way to describe it. He had a unique setup with a floor tom-tom on the left side of the drum set, which means it was adjacent to the hi-hat. He did these fancy cross-overs with his sticks, and it was very effective. It reminded me of what I've seen timpani players do in the symphony, where they cross their arms over to play certain passages. I was so lucky—even though it was winter and snowing, I waited outside the stage door for Mr. Jones, and when he came out, he was so nice. He looked like Mr. Class, with the elegant overcoat and hat, and he was so friendly and answered my question. I asked him if he had a tom-tom on the left because he used to play timpani in school.

And he said, "Exactly, my friend. You are very smart. I learned how to cross stick on the timpani and thought I would apply it to the drum set. That is exactly where I got it."

I said, "It's one of the great original things you've brought to your playing." And then I asked him about his hi-hat cymbals, and he told me they were 13-inch, and he told me they were medium on the top and a heavier one on the bottom. He was just as helpful as a person could be. I told him what a privilege it was to talk with him, and he said, "That's okay, young blood." He called a lot of the young guys "young blood."

Can you imagine, about fifteen years after that, he called me as his sub with Joe Bushkin at the Embers Club in New York City. Boy, it brings tears to my eyes as I think about subbing for one of these great, great players. It meant so much to me. Many of us call him the father of modern drumming—he got away from a lot of the press rolls and heavy stuff and went to a lighter, more swinging style. Max Roach had a great saying: "Out of every three drum beats we play, we owe two to Jo Jones."

Roy Haynes   I admired him immensely, although I would say he has come into his own in the last twenty years—and he's 84 years old. In some ways, he was a bit overshadowed by the very large presences of Max Roach and Art Blakey. Roy Haynes was a fine figure and a fine drummer, but spending as long as he did with Sarah Vaughan, for instance, he wasn't quite in the front lines of the straight jazz bands. Roy got a lot better in later years. He was great to begin with, but he played stronger and more aggressively later.

He was a lighter player; they were more dynamic. They played a little louder and more dynamic, but he played wonderfully in his manner, and he was very original. I'm glad everyone has discovered Roy Haynes in the last twenty years. And he's still playing great. He's one of my favorite people; he's a fun, fun man. I just think he's the cat's meow, and he's still going strong, God bless him. I love Roy Haynes.

Shelly Manne   I remember the terrific impression I got of Shelly Manne in a Coast Guard uniform when I was about fifteen, and he sat in at the Down Beat Club. He picked up a pair of brushes, and he played with such an almost elegant motion. He got a great pulse when he played. Certainly the sound is the first thing you talk about. He got a great bursting pulse, but mostly he was so smooth. He had a rather unique way of playing the brushes. It's hard to verbally describe it, but everything flowed. I was really impressed with his approach to brushes. Of course, he had a very swinging and graceful manner when he played with sticks too, without a doubt, but his brush playing was quite unique.

Shelly Manne was always very helpful when I'd ask him questions. In fact, when I was with Charlie Ventura, and I was getting myself a pretty good reputation, he came down to see me at the Royal Roost and said, "Eddie, you're doing some great stuff on the drums, but you sit so low that nobody can see a damn thing you're doing." I was, at that time, sitting very low, which became popular later with all the rock guys, but most of the jazz guys sat higher. Because he said that to me, I raised my seat. I didn't even have a drum throne at that time. I was sitting on a drum case with a pillow. I guess I got myself another pillow, or maybe I got a drum seat, but I definitely started sitting a little higher. Shelly said, "Believe me, why should you waste all that great visual stuff you're doing?" No one had ever been nice enough to tell me that before.

I'll also never forget that when I was broke, Shelly gave me some brushes. I was amazed because he wrapped some moleskin around the handles for a good grip—they were metal brushes, and most of us found they were slippery. Later, they started making rubber on the brushes for a better grip.

I was so broke that I couldn't buy brushes, and all the bristles had fallen out. You can't repair them. I happened to mention that to Shelly, and although I wasn't asking for brushes, he said, "Wait a minute—I have three old pair," and he gave me two of the pairs, which lasted me a year. I thought that was so great.

I remember one time saying to him, "Boy, you play in some bands, and some guys can really be a drag, you know?" And he said to me, "I'm going to tell you a mantra for your life. You will never keep sixteen people happy. I don't care who you are, and I don't care how you play. There will be somebody who doesn't care for what you're doing, but what's important is that you're doing your best. If you have the majority on your side, you're ahead of the game.' I never forgot that: "You'll never keep sixteen people happy." It was good advice.

When I told him that when I was younger, I would get excited and push the tempo a little bit, he said another profound thing to me: "Everybody does. I did that too, but you know what happens, Eddie? Good time becomes a habit." I love that phrase. He said, "I honestly don't think anyone has perfect time"—and he was known to have very good time. He could take one second or two seconds off a thirty-second commercial. I could, too. That's good time.

I asked, "The more you concentrate on good time, the more it gets into you?"

"As long as you're concentrating on it," he said. "You know when you were younger, you used to push it." I said, "'Yeah, but I think I'm out of that now."

I heard Shelly play with Stan Kenton, and he was an equally gifted small-band drummer.

Kenny Clarke As I got older and learned a little more and heard a lot more, I realized how many drummers, from Max Roach to Roy Haynes and Art Blakey, were influenced by Kenny Clarke. I don't mean that they never gave Kenny credit—they did—but I was a little unaware for a while, frankly, of how much influence Kenny had, because Max became such a dominating figure of the bop era, along with Blakey.

But here's the deal with Kenny Clarke—or "Klook," as he was known, … I snuck into the Onyx Club during my teenage years (when I was sixteen or seventeen). It was on the north side of 52nd Street and not easy to get in. Somehow, though, I got by the doorman and stood in a dark corner. I heard a remarkable thing: Kenny Clarke playing a four-piece drum set—bass drum, snare drum, hi-hat, ride cymbal, and a rather small ride cymbal for those days. The cymbals were getting bigger with the be-bop era; they were getting up to 20, 21, and 22 inches. The guys in Kenton's band were playing 24's (except Shelly; he wouldn't do that).

Klook had a cymbal that I don't think was bigger than 17 inches or at the max, 18 inches, and it sat up there rather flat. We were all playing them at an angle because it was easier to play fast at an angle. It certainly didn't slow down Klook , but the main thing is, when he started to play with Tadd Dameron's quartet (Tadd Dameron was a great pianist, arranger, and composer; a terrifically original voice of the bop era), he began to play on this funny little cymbal, and the total sound coming out of not just the cymbal but his whole set was so musical. I almost think it was the most musical sound I've ever heard— it was the way he had them tuned and, of course, 80 percent was the way he played. He had a great touch.

He had a way of playing the hi-hat with the foot in rhythm that was unique. He sort of danced on it with his toe, a la Tony Williams, who later also danced with his toe. But unlike Tony Williams, who played sort of a straight 4/4 and very well, Kenny actually played four beats to the bar by closing the cymbals with the foot only—no hands, no sticks—and he actually sounded

48

like a rhythm guitar, because he had a little after-beat built in. I've tried to do it, but I can't even get close. He would dance with his toe on the hi-hat while he played the ride cymbal, and you would hear ch, CH, ch, CH, ch, CH,

I once sat right next to him at a little club called the Downbeat Club, over near 8th Avenue in the 50s. I happened to be sitting with my ear practically in Kenny's hi-hat, and that's when I really became aware of what a sophisticated technique he had going. It wasn't just a straight after-beat like the rest of us idiots were playing. I remember leaving that night thinking, "Will wonders never cease? There's always something to learn when you're listening to great players." I've never heard anybody else do that.

People like Tadd Dameron, who had a good ear for drums and everything else, used Kenny Clarke a lot because he could play ensemble figures, and of course his comping was spectacular. Many people feel that after Jo Jones, Kenny Clarke was the original comper. Sometimes I think he didn't get quite the recognition that he deserves, and one of the reasons is he got tired of racial prejudice—this what he told me himself when I saw him in Paris; he had moved to Europe and worked in Europe most of the time. He was such a talented guy. I think he also played rather good piano. People should pay a lot of attention to Klook. He also had a pulse that was such dynamite. I have a theory that there's nothing like hearing a person in person. I don't care what it is that person plays; I like to hear the sound the person makes in person, before the engineers and the dials start screwing around. That's why hearing Kenny Clarke was such a pleasure. He had such a musical sound when he played the drums. If there is an epitome of a musical drummer, it is Kenny Clarke, for sure.

Don Lamond   Don was a friend and neighbor, and I loved his drumming. He lived two blocks away from me in Massapequa, Long Island, during my first marriage. I liked him so much that I sold him my boat for two hundred dollars when I went to California, and he, in return, gave me a great painting called Mother and Child that I still have hanging in my house.

Long before I met him, I admired the hell out of his work. Around 1946 he made famous records with Woody Herman called "Four Brothers," and he did a slower blues called "I've Got News for You," where he played some stunning double-time breaks. He did some drum breaks that drummers are still trying to figure out. He really became "flavor of the month"—I hate the term, but I'm using it in a positive manner. But Don, really, was "flavor of the year" for a couple of years. The interesting thing is that Don never played long drum solos. He was famous for short little bursts, short little breaks, but he made them memorable, and he didn't play like most other drummers. Later, I found out why. He said, "Once I learned how to play, when I practiced, I didn't practice rudimental strokes like most drummers. I practiced musical phrases on my practice pad or drum, as played by Charlie Parker and Dizzy Gillespie at that time, the two leading be-bop lights."

That's why when he played drum breaks, he didn't sound like anybody else. He got a really popping sound out of the bass drum. He did things like putting shredded newspaper inside the bass drum, and he'd shake it up to get it to lay against the drum heads just the way he liked. He also cut off the beater to the bass drum at an angle so it was flat and therefore got a flatter sound out of the bass drum—not as much of a boomy sound. I personally think through he's been somewhat ignored the years. Except for that time in the '40s, I don't think he's been given due that he should have received. Even today, sixty years later, if you play some of those records, he still sounds unique and different. I think that uniqueness is what is prized, especially with a jazz drummer. I think he was one of the leading lights of that kind of thing. He had a great sense of time and really knew how to do it with a band, but he didn't quite do it the way everybody else, including me, did it. Where you thought he might play a fill, leading into a figure, he wouldn't. And in a place where maybe you wouldn't, he would. But it always sounded great.

"Unconventional" was the description given by Lou Levy, a fine pianist with Woody Herman. He said, "Don always surprised us. Where you expected the guy to play a little setup into a figure, he didn't. And then maybe right after the figure, he'd play something and you'd say, isn't that great." So he had that very original thing. In his book *Good Vibes*, Terry Gibbs actually said the 1946–47 band was Don Lamond's band. He meant it in a good way, not that he played too much or that he took it over. It's just that he was so strong a stylist that he marked the band with something very different and unique at that time. He was a lovely guy, but because of his type of face, he got the nickname "Hound Dog" when he was younger. I thought he was a nice-looking man, but guys in the early bands called him that and it stuck. Don Lamond also loved to do cartoon voices: "I taut I taw a putty tat." And I'd ask him to do that. He had sort of a down-home twang, and he was a down-home kind of a guy. That's what I liked about him. He was very different from a great many musicians. He was very hip, but he didn't care about being hip. He kept his roots. I still think he was very underrated. I tell all my students about him and when they hear him, they say, "Oh, man, that's sure different." When things slowed down in the '60s, Don became the drummer at Walt Disney World for close to fifteen years.

Buddy Rich: The Many Sides of Buddy Rich

I was probably seventeen years old the first time I saw Buddy Rich. I had already heard the great icons of the be-bop era and the swing era. I had heard Max, and Art, and Kenny Clarke, and Gene Krupa, and Jo Jones, and Big Sid Catlett, and Davey Tough. I first heard Buddy Rich playing with the Tommy Dorsey band at the Paramount Theater. As usual, I took my lunch of two sandwiches in a brown paper bag and got myself up at 6:00 in the morning so I could get a good seat. The Paramount would show a movie, and then present a well-known big band, usually a singer, a tap dancer, and maybe a juggler and a comedian.

Dorsey's band came up, and Buddy was playing his ass off. Like anybody else who had never before seen Buddy Rich before—although I had heard him on records, of course—I was just flabbergasted. His overall command of the drum set was, without a doubt, the greatest I had ever seen. The sense of propulsion, drive, and swing were remarkable. And the most remarkable thing of all was that he played a drum solo on his feature "Not So Quiet, Please" that was fantastic. I couldn't believe it. Like most people, when I heard him play, it was unbelievable because he was doing things so beyond what any other drummer could play. It was not so much his display of technique—which many people laud him for; that's true. It was that he was creative. My friend Kenny and I suffered through the movie that day. One of us went to the can while the other watched the seat. We ate our sandwiches and watched the movie the second time, and then up came the Dorsey band. The remarkable thing was that on Buddy Rich's solo of the same tune, his playing was completely different from the first show. I mean, completely different. The only thing he repeated was the cue for the band to come in, which was a very fast single stroke. I had heard a lot of drummers play solos, but I also found out, after hearing them three or four times, that they tended to go to the same places most of the time. That doesn't mean it wasn't good, but Rich played in a truly creative jazz style. He created something completely new each time. This was a revelation to me. I think people were so overwhelmed with his technique that they forgot to talk about that.

I stayed for three shows. On the third show, he played differently than he had on the first two shows, and I walked out of there completely mesmerized. I said, "This guy has not only the greatest ability on the drum set, as far as the technical command, but he plays so creatively, in a true jazz manner. And he doesn't play it safe by having any kind of routine."

Of course, I became enamored of Buddy Rich, like everybody, although I will say I was already strongly under the influence of all the other drummers I've mentioned. Therefore, I wasn't about to try to become a Buddy Rich clone, which many guys did, really unsuccessfully. Buddy Rich used to say, "There's nothing worse than a bad imitation." And he was so right. The best thing to do is, like Charlie Parker said, "Play yourself; be yourself." I had already had enough influences from other kinds of players, like Sidney Catlett, Jo Jones, Max, Davey Tough, Kenny Clarke, and Art Blakey, that whatever package I was putting together was going to be a composite of those influences and something original too, I hoped.

My very first actual encounter with Buddy Rich was when I was seventeen and working at a beat-up old 9th Avenue club with a trio—a tenor player named Louie from Brooklyn, and a piano player. I broke my last stick and had to tape it, but that doesn't work once the stick is broken. I was broke and couldn't buy a new one. I said, "Louie, I faked the ending of the last set, but

I'm really stuck here. What am I going to do?"

He said, "Ah, it's cool. I grew up with Buddy Rich in Brooklyn. Buddy's at the Paramount around the corner." The Paramount was something like 44th Street and we were at 45th and 9th. He said, "I won't start the set until you come back." I ran over from 9th Street and went to the stage door and said, "I have a message for Buddy from Lou from Brooklyn." The guy called up to Buddy, "The guy says he has a message from Lou from Brooklyn."

"All right," Buddy answered. He came down in a silk dressing gown, looking very classy, and said, "You're working with Lou? Give Lou my best. That's one of my buddies from Brooklyn. Nice to meet you, kid."

I said, "Mr. Rich, I'm so embarrassed. I don't know how to say this …" "What's the matter?" he asked.

"I broke my last drumsticks. Could you loan me a pair of drumsticks? I'm so embarrassed." He said, "Don't be silly. Everybody's been there." He called the band boy over and told him something, and the guy went away. Buddy asked me, "Do you go to school, son?"

I said, "I just finished high school." And he said, "Good for you, and you're playing already." He asked more questions, and then the guy came back with a brown bag, and Buddy said, "That's ten pair of sticks. That'll hold you for a while."

I said, "Oh, Mr. Rich, I can't thank you enough."

He said, "Don't be silly. I get them by the hundreds."

"I'll never forget this, Mr. Rich," I told him.

He said, "Don't you even mention this, kid." It chokes me up even now to think of that. When I reminded him, years later, that he'd done that, he denied that he would have done it. He said, "You're gonna kill my image." But I knew there were times he gave drum sets to kids whose drum sets burned up or were stolen.

The next major time I spent with him was when I was in my twenties, and I was working at Birdland. I went down on a Monday night to hear my friend Charlie Mingus and his band. As I walked down into the club, there was Buddy Rich, sitting with a guy right at a table near the entrance. We had met once or twice, but he said, "Hey, Ed, come and sit with me." I said, "Okay, Buddy, thanks." When I sat down, he said, "What is that crap up there on the stage?"

That got my Irish up. I said, "What is that crap? That's my friend Charlie Mingus. He's one of the most talented guys we have in music today. He writes all his own music. He's a virtuoso bass player. What's the matter with you?"

The other guy, who I found out later was an agent, said, "You can't talk to Buddy Rich like that."

Buddy looked at him and said, "You take a walk." And then Buddy said to me, "Okay, you know what? I'm going to sit here and pay attention."

I was really boiling because Charlie was a friend of mine, not just a great musician, so I said, "Yeah, maybe you can pay attention for a change."

He listened for a few minutes and then said, "You know what? You're right. The guy is really right. You know, kid, I like the way you stuck up for your friend." He put his hand out and said, "I think we're going to get along real good."

It gives me chills when I think about it. That's really when we became friends. He came to my house in New York for dinner a few times.

One time he came in his sports car and picked me up on the corner of 52nd Street, and we drove out to Long Island, where he was playing with his band. I was wearing an orange baseball cap, and as he drove up in his convertible, I saw he was wearing an orange baseball cap, too—he thought that meant something. He said, "Man, far out. Dig that—we're both wearing an orange baseball cap."

We first went to my parents-in-law's house in Port Jefferson for a picnic lunch, and then Buddy went to play an outdoor concert. I went to see him in his dressing room at intermission, and I happened to walk in just as he was kicking in the screen of a television and yelling at his band boy because he couldn't get the Jackie Gleason Show that he had taped a day or two before—he'd wanted to see himself on Jackie Gleason. I said, "That's really gonna help, Buddy."

And he was yelling, "Well, God damn it, it doesn't get any reception. I told you to get a set that works!"

And the poor boy said, "Buddy, I went to rental store and got a TV, and they said with the rabbit ears, you'd get a picture. What do I know?"

Buddy was fit to be tied, so I left. But we had had a nice day until then. He was very mercurial. And after intermission, he played nothing but loud, fast songs. My wife said to me, "Don't you think he ought to change the pace?" And I said, "I think I know why he won't."

I saw him play with a broken arm twice and play drum solos one-handed. He just used a foot like another hand—nobody will ever be able to do that again. When Louie Bellson was getting too much publicity with Tommy Dorsey for using two bass drums, Buddy had two bass drums made on a platform. At the Paramount Theater, he sat on a seat with those two bass drums and nothing else, and he played a drum solo with nothing but his feet—he broke up the place. I remember the tune was "Ol' Man River.' No hands. You know, he was a good tap dancer, so you can only imagine.

Buddy Rich: The Famous Drum Battle (or Liar, Liar)

In 1972, Buddy Rich and I talked the *Tonight Show* into a drum duet, or drum battle, which people liked to call it (although we called it a duet). Of course, Johnny Carson is the one who okayed it, because it takes quite a bit of a setup because of the lighting and the microphones for drum sets and two drummers. We had been trying to do it for a little while, and I finally asked Johnny personally, and he gave his okay. The way Buddy and I figured it was that we would sit and rehearse with Doc Severinsen's band, but we wouldn't play any solos during the rehearsal—there was no need for that. Buddy said, "What would you like to do?"

And I said, "Why don't we both play together with the band when the arrangement starts and when they stop in the middle for us guys, you start out and play for a short time, and then I'll play for a short time, and then you play for a short time, and then I'll play for a short time—maybe we'll do that three times. You do three, I'll do three, and then I'll start a signal and look over to you, and you join in. And you give a count in to Doc, because you're closer to Doc than I am, and we'll bring the band in, and that'll be it."

He said, "That sounds good." He was very easy to work with on stuff like that, very relaxed. (Why wouldn't he be, with his gifts?)

So we had our rehearsal, but we just said to Doc, "We're going to do our stuff in this thing," and I gave him the cue for the ending. Buddy joined me, and the band came in at the rehearsal, and that way Doc knew exactly how to bring the band in and out. Before the show, I went into the dressing room to talk to Buddy.

By this time, Buddy was a very close friend of mine—he'd been to my house for dinner and played with the kids. In fact, my wife always said he was "the nicest dinner guest" you could have. That was the very warm side of Buddy that some people never saw, but we saw it.

So I said to him, "Now look, we're friends. Of course I want you to play good. I know you're going to play good, but don't get out there and start doing some of that tricky stuff that nobody can possibly do. Then you're going to make me look like nothing, you know?"

He said, "Ah, don't worry. You have nothing to worry about; it'll be fine. I wouldn't do that to you." "Okay, I'm just telling you," I said. "You got a lot of great stuff, but don't bring out a lot of super-duper stuff, you know? One hand under, one hand over and around your neck, and everything else that other guys like me can't do." "Don't worry about; it'll be fine," he said.

So, when it came time for the two drummers to get out there, Johnny made the announcement: "Buddy and Ed are going to do a drum battle." And we start up. Buddy played his short first thing; I played my short first thing. Buddy played his second short thing …but on my second short thing, I must have made some kind of move where I ran around the drums kinda fast, and for the very first time, the audience applauded loudly. That was all Buddy had to see and hear!

On his last go-around—man, he pulled out the heaviest stuff he could do, with the left hand over the right hand, the left hand under the right hand and moving around, and doing some stuff, like I said originally, that only he could do. Obviously, he got super applause.

And I was laughing. When I started my last time around, instead of trying to compete with that—which no one could do—I just clicked the sticks up high, like a stick trick, with a smile, and then started the signal like, "Let's go," and he joined me. And the band came in, and we finished it fine together.

I went back to the dressing room after the show and said to him, "Hey, old friend, whatever happened to our deal? You pulled out some of the hardest stuff that you do, the trickiest stuff that nobody can match. Thanks a lot!"

And he looked at me and said, with mock sincerity, "You know, I just got carried away."

I wouldn't have had it any other way, though. It was sort of right that he should always show that he had that super element that made him so great, and it was fun anyway. It was Buddy being Buddy, really. Thanks, Buddy. I miss ya like crazy, pal; I really do. Life was a lot more fun and inspiring when you were around.

OTHER DRUMMERS

I've already referred to some of the older guys—my peers, the guys I grew up listening to—but I want to mention some drummers I think a great deal of. There are three groups. The first group consists of guys twenty-five to thirty years younger than me, but don't forget—I'm eighty-two, so they are in their fifties or early sixties and all play beautifully. The second group will be much younger guys, some of whom are fairly new on the scene, that I've had a chance to hear and the third consists of two recent hearings.

THE MIDDLE GUARD

Bob Moses　　　I want to mention my godchild, Bob Moses, who is a very talented drummer and composer. There is hardly anything this guy doesn't do. I've been his godfather since he was about ten years old. I knew his parents, Dick and Greta Moses, very well in New York. Bob's given me credit for starting him out in music, although I think he would have found music by himself. I did take him around to jazz clubs when he was twelve, and he loved Charlie Mingus, and I think I took him to see Bird. He got very captivated by jazz. I gave him a small drum set and he started to play. Later on, I gave him a set of vibes, and I think that helped him develop his melodic qualities, because he started composing and arranging. He's made albums where he wrote all the music for the band. He's very talented and very original. He's played with eminent people like Gary Burton and Steve Swallow and a laundry list of fine people through the years. Then he took the invitation from the New England

55

Conservatory to teach drum set there, and he's been up there for many years. He's still playing, though, which is great. He's a very talented fellow. We are yet to hear even more from him as time goes on, because he's more than just a fine player. He's extremely original in the way he composes music. I'm lucky in having such a talented guy as a godson.

Jeff Hamilton   Jeff is a marvelous, remarkable drummer with a great, great melodic sense. He has a fine sense of swing. I used him years ago on the Tonight Show as my sub when he was a pretty young guy, and believe me, that was not an easy chair to find a sub for, because the sub had to play everything well. We struck out a few times, trying to find a sub. I'd used my great friend Nick Ceroli as my sub, but when he passed, I was so happy to find Jeff—Doc liked him, and the band liked him, and he did a great job. Since then, of course, he's gone on to fantastic things, with a long stint with Ray Brown, as co-leader with the Clayton-Hamilton Jazz Orchestra, one of our greatest ensembles, and now he's also very busy with the Jeff Hamilton Trio. He's done a great job playing in both the trio and small-band and big-band concept. Not too many guys are good at both.

Joe La Barbera   Joe is a great friend of mine and another person who plays wonderful big-band and also small-group drumming. Joe first came to fame with the Bill Evans Trio. He has that sensitivity and response and overall musical playing that blended so very well with Bill Evans. He moved on to the Woody Herman Band and so many other wonderful musical situations, like with Tony Bennett. He has been more or less freelance for some years now, and he teaches at California Institute of the Arts (Cal Arts.) Joe has a wonderful style—all the gentlemen in this "middle guard" and the younger guys have their own styles, which I respect a great deal.

    Joe is also a wonderful personal friend. He lives not too far from me and has been a very good friend, especially during my wife's illness. I can't mention how many times he's come through for me. He has two talented brothers: Pat, a wonderful tenor player; and John, one of our premier composer/ arrangers—they are equally as great as people as Joe is. It's a wonderful family– the La Barbera family. I am happy to know them, and I love them all.

Peter Erskine   Peter has shown he can play everything from hard rock to music like Weather Report and Maynard Ferguson and many big bands. He is one of our most versatile players, extremely musical, and he's done a lot of work similar to what I've done in my career, in that he's played with symphonic orchestras and such. In addition to that, he's a good composer—far beyond any writing that I've ever done—and has composed for dance as well as concert music. He's a wonderfully well-rounded musician and brings a great sound and conception to all of his drumming. He's great fun to see and hear.

THE YOUNG GUARD

Eric Harland   Eric plays mostly with the San Francisco Collective Group, which is an all-star band that has done some very wonderful things. He's played with many other people, but I think he's best known for that. He's a very musical drummer. I think I heard him first on a record with Terence Blanchard, which is when I first started paying attention to him.

Kendrick Scott   Kendrick Scott is now with Terence Blanchard. I had the pleasure of teaching him one summer at Skidmore Jazz Institute. He was a great student. He played wonderfully well then, and he was only a young guy of about sixteen. He's since gone on to quite a bit of fame and a lot of wonderful drumming.

Justin Faulkner   Justin started at about age eighteen with Branford Marsalis, and now he's an old man of maybe nineteen. He plays great. He has a different style—his own individual style—and swings really good and has a lot of energy. I know Branford is thrilled to have him—he calls Justin a "drumming demon."

TWO RECENT HEARINGS

Two great drummers are **Bill Stewart** and **Greg Hutchinson**. Both are playing absolutely top-level contemporary drums. Hearing Greg recently with John Scofield was a thrilling experience.

GUITAR PLAYERS I'D LIKE TO MENTION

Mundell Lowe   Mundell was a very good friend of mine in New York. I worked on and off with him over a period of ten years, at least. One of the fun things I did with him was a trio, along with the great George Duvivier on bass. The Today Show used us as intermission music. We would sometimes play at Birdland until 3:00 in the morning, go have breakfast, and show up at 6:00 a.m. for the Today Show at NBC—and then go home and sleep. A lot of times after breakfast, we'd have to sit around, waiting to play on the television show. I really envied George because he could sit in a straight chair and doze off for five minutes. I'd say, "Okay, George, we're gonna play," and he'd wake up and be as fresh as a daisy. I thought that was a great thing. He was a master of catnaps. He could drive from coast to coast the way some people would fly because he used catnaps. He'd drive four or five hundred miles, pull over to the side of the road, take a tiny nap, and then keep going.

I made three or four albums with Mundell. Through working with him, I worked for the first time with the great pianist Bill Evans. A lot of people don't know that Bill Evans was a fine flute player, too. I think he gave up the instrument in later years, but when I worked with him in a couple of clubs in Jersey with Mundell, he played some excellent flute, as well as, of course, fantastic piano. I made a very interesting album with Bill Evans, with arrangements by Gary McFarland, a talented young writer whom we lost much too young. He scored an album for Bill Evans with string section and rhythm section called The Gary McFarland Orchestra—Featuring Bill Evans. It's one of the albums I'm most proud of, because it's just so quality.

Mundell has a very individual style. He has a touch of the old, meaning he knows who Charlie Christian was and great players of that era, and yet he sounds very modern. I think as a rhythm guitarist—which he doesn't do a lot of, because he's a solo guitarist—he can play closest to the famous Freddie Green with Count Basie; that I know. He's got that same feel and sound that Freddie had, and I think that's something that should be noted. Not many people can do that.

Johnny Smith Johnny's name is not as well known today, but among guitarists, he's still very well known. His recordings of "Moonlight in Vermont" and things like that are considered guitar classics. Even young guitarists buy those albums. He had a way of playing chords and things that was very unique. He retired rather early and went out West, where he had a ranch and flew cattle and bulls around in an airplane. He did a lot of studio work, but he was a very fine jazz player, and he just packed it in. I worked a lot with him.

Wes Montgomery   I made an album with Wes when he was making records for the first time. He was phenomenally great with the thumb—he didn't use a pick. He was a most interesting musician to play with. I tended to play a little more quietly because his using his thumb wasn't as strident of a sound as with a pick. I remember when someone asked Wes to play a tune in 5/4 rhythm, he said, "I've never played a tune in 5/4 rhythm in my life." But he was told, "It would be good if you could do this in 5/4, because it would be very unique."

The bass player on that date, Richard Davis, recently called me and reminded me, "Do you remember how you saved the day with Wes?"

And I said, "No, what did I do?"

And he said, "You said, 'Look, Wes, Richard and I will get a little 5/4 rhythm going, and you'll see how it feels and if you can play a little. If you hate it, we won't do it.' We started playing, and Wes began to play as if he had been playing 5/4 all his life. The guy yelled, 'Roll the tape,' and we made the tune, and it came out just fine."

George Benson   I made a couple of albums with him. He's famous for singing, but he's a great guitarist too. I remember the first album I made with him, called *White Rabbit*. I said, "George, you sound so good playing. Do you get a chance to play as much as you want lately?"

"No, they're sticking me up in front of the microphone," he said. "If you want to know the truth, they don't know what to do with me. I can sing pretty good."

"You sing very good," I said.

"Yeah, but I'm a player at heart."

"Yeah, but they're telling you there's bigger bucks in singing," I said. He said, "Yeah, they are." So he found a way to do both.

Chuck Wayne Chuck was a wonderful player and very original. I worked a lot with him. We used to have a little group with him, George, and me. George and I were like a little rhythm team, and many people would hire both of us because we played well together. Chuck was a fine player and a wonderful guy to work with.

YOUR HIT PARADE

Your Hit Parade was the No.1 most popular show in the 1950s. Raymond Scott, who was a notoriously eccentric bandleader, was the bandleader for the show. For my audition, he had me come up to his office with a snare drum and stand and a pair of brushes. He said, "Okay, sit down and play as fast as you can."

I said, "What do you mean, play as fast as I can? Do you want a drum solo?"

He said, "No, not a drum solo, just play the fastest tempo you can play and keep going for quite a while."

Being that I was quite an expert at that stuff from playing all the bebop tunes so fast, I started humming "Cherokee" to give myself something to do other than just tippy-tap. I did it for about two choruses and then stopped.

He said, "That's very good. Okay, I want to hire you and make you the percussionist on the Lucky Strike Hit Parade."

And I thought, "Then why the hell do you have me up here playing snare drum fast as I can?" I don't know—maybe he thought he had a drummer in reserve if, God forbid, Cliff Leeman, the drummer, got ill. But in any case, he hired me, and it was a good job because I needed more experience on those other instruments. He had heard me play conga drums with Peggy Lee in a nightclub, and he thought I played very good conga. I played good conga, but I don't know about very good conga. I played good conga and good bongos—my Puerto Rican friends taught me in New York, and I'd give them drum set tips. Raymond really wanted to add the conga and bongo sounds to the Lucky Strike Hit Parade on some tunes, not all tunes.

I was a good timpanist and my mallet work was mediocre, but he didn't care about that. I said, "I play these Latin drums good. I play timpani good, but if you want an expert mallet player, don't hire me."

He said, "That's the last thing I care about. If you get a part on vibes or xylophone that's too hard, you can simplify it," which is what I did. The mallet parts were just a little extra whipped cream in the arrangements. They never wrote the mallet parts to be important. I had an okay situation there.

The timpani were set on the back on the floor of the bandstand. The bandstand was raised, with Cliff on the drums, and all the other guys were up higher. I was alongside of them on the floor level. Where the timpani were placed toward the rear of the bandstand on the floor and where I sat when I didn't have something to play was a little corridor that looked onto the dancing girls' changing room. They had a gauze curtain up that probably looked opaque from the side they were changing on, but from my side, I could see everything that went on inside the changing room. Obviously, to a young buck in heat, it was really great to see those gorgeous, leggy chorus girls changing clothes.

I would count my measure before I had to come in to play timpani, and I had to move my stool back six inches so it wasn't very obvious that I was looking. No one knew it—but Cliff knew it. And if I was ever late on my timpani entrance, he would laugh his ass off and say, "Eddie, you're watching the chicks too long." He got a big kick out of it. He was a wonderful man and one of the finest people I've ever known in the music business—a very classy guy. He got such a kick out of the fact that Eddie could move his chair back six inches and watch the girls get semi-nudie, changing outfits. I really missed him when he passed away some years after that.

Cliff was very popular at traditional jazz festivals. Musicians loved him; he had a musical touch. He played Your Hit Parade with bass drum, snare drum, hi-hats, and one cymbal about 16 inches, which he never used as a ride cymbal, not for that kind of music. He felt that closer, tighter sounds fit that poppy-poppy-woppy music, so he played everything with sticks on the hi-hat, mostly closed, and of course brushes. He did a great job and would swing the band really good.

I learned a lot down below with my percussion stuff from hearing him play, because he was such a finished drummer. He never played more than was needed. He knew how to play for the music and never tried to sell himself. Your Hit Parade was the forerunner of the today's Top 20, Top 40, Top 10. It featured the songs that were played the most on the radio. The challenge was that the song would stay popular for a long time, and they had to make it newly exciting the next week. It was a very popular show. I want to especially give credit to Cliff for being so great.

Raymond Scott was just a character. I got along okay with him, like I did with all the other characters, but the most famous story about him was that he was married to a lovely girl named Dorothy Collins. She was a good singer and did Broadway a few times. He would have her sing a song while she got down on her knees on the ground and picked up marbles off the floor with her mouth. If this is true—although it was printed in an eminent national magazine—it is the wackiest thing I've ever heard. He thought this would help her concentrate more on her singing if she had to do something else at the same time. I never had the nerve to ask Dorothy, but one time I said to her, "Boy, Raymond is a real character," and she said, "You should only know." She did divorce him later on. She was a sweetheart of a girl.

EDDIE CONDON AND CLIFF LEEMAN

The great drummer Cliff Leeman, who was on the show Your Hit Parade, where I was hired as a percussionist, was a prince among men. He was an idol of a lot of us young musicians, because when he was with the Casa Loma Orchestra, the word on the street was that he was the lover of Betty George, the band's singer. Betty was an absolutely impossibly beautiful girl, with Elizabeth Taylor coloring of black hair and blue eyes, and a Sophia Loren figure. To us, Cliff Leeman had to be a successful man because he was boffing Betty George. Cliff, by the way, was very handsome himself and loaded with charm, so nothing came as a surprise in that area. He was a great drummer and played with Charlie Barnett, Artie Shaw, and Tommy Dorsey. As an older drummer— he was 20 years older than I was—he did not resent a young up-and-coming drummer like me. He did not have any of that in him at all. He was like Mo Goldenberg and Louie Bellson and people who wanted to help people and who weren't worried about competition.

During the 1950s, Cliff and I were working on the *Lucky Strike Hit Parade* at NBC, which featured the top ten tunes at that time. I was playing percussion, like bongos and congas, and Cliff was the drummer. We got to be very friendly and after a short time he said, "How about you subbing for me for the two weeks I take off from Eddie Condon's?" Eddie Condon was a world-famous figure at the time. He had his own club, Condon's, and his own TV show at times.

I said, "Oh, gee, what a nice thing for you to do. Do you think I'll be okay?"

He said, "I know you. You can play everything. You went to Europe with Benny Goodman—the test of fire. You'll be fine."

And I was fine; I was okay. But what was thrilling about playing at Eddie Condon's was that first of all Eddie Condon was a wonderful guy, and he played great rhythm guitar. He could really swing on rhythm guitar. He was a historical raconteur. He had a sly and dry wit, and he could keep you laughing. You almost wet your pants sometimes, he was so funny. He knew the name of every song; he knew who balled who in what year; he knew the brand of liquor that people drank—he was just a fun man, and he treated me great. And in the band, I was playing alongside the purist bass player Walter Page, known as Big 'Un, because he was so big. Jo Jones, the great drummer, had said, "I learned how to play drums from Big 'Un." Big 'Un and I hit it off. He was certainly twenty or twenty-five years older than I, and we made a deal every other night, where one of us would buy a pint of bourbon and split it. We had such fun, because we never got loaded; we'd just have a few shots in between sets. He was such a fun man. I would always ask him stories about the Basie band because he was part of the original, historic Count Basie Band of the '30s, and I thought that was just great.

Also in the band was a famous trumpeter named Wild Bill Davidson, the biggest name in traditional music at that time. He was like the white Louie Armstrong, if there were such a thing. On trombone was Cutty Cutshall, a great name in that field, and on clarinet was one of the pioneers of that style of music, Edmond Hall. That was the typical front line of the traditional band: trumpet, trombone, and clarinet. They're still playing like that in New Orleans today—plus, of course, bass, drums, and piano. In the olden days there would have been tuba and drums and banjo. On piano, there was a great pianist named Gene Schroeder, who was one of two or three of the best in that style. When I played with them, I was playing with the crème de la crème of that style.

The fact that Charlie Parker and Dizzy Gillespie were making history across town in different clubs had nothing to do with this music. They played this music with the tradition that it was played, and they played it great. They played the older tunes like "Struttin' with Some Barbecue," and they played it with what is called Chicago style– definitely with a 4/4 feeling, no two-beat stuff, no boom chuck, boom chuck. It was good, swinging 4/4 feeling, the way Davey Tough used to play that stuff out in Chicago with Bud Freeman and Eddie Condon and those guys. That's where that feel really started, I've been told; it was with those guys out in Chicago, as opposed to the two-beat feel that more of the New Orleans musicians played earlier.

Eddie Condon asked me to do that. For drummers to learn all their arrangements would be equally as hard as learning be-bop arrangements. There are a lot of stops and goes, a lot of accents, but luckily I had heard a lot of that music, and I managed to do pretty well. They liked me enough to say to Cliff, "You can bring the kid back next summer."

Once in a while Johnny Carson would come down and sit in on drums, long before I was working with him. Sometimes I could get him up to play if he was feeling extra good; sometimes I couldn't. In later years on the Tonight Show, I could never get him to play. He said to me, "I had to have about four drinks before I'd get up to play, and I don't have four drinks when I'm doing the Tonight Show."

I liked that period of time. Guys who were playing modern music didn't understand. They had their horns up their asses, saying, "How do you go play with those old guys?"

I said, "You're full of it. They play their old stuff as good as you play your stuff, maybe better. Stop being critical. Have you ever really sat down and listened? You only know flavor of the month."

I thought it was an honor that at age twenty-six or twenty-seven I was allowed to play with these great giants. They were all giant names in their field. I was very indebted to Cliff for the opportunity. And I think I ended up doing three summers for him, two weeks at a time.

OLIVER NELSON

One of the most rewarding associations I had in the '60s was with the great Oliver Nelson, a premier composer, arranger, and wonderful saxophonist, whether on tenor or alto. I had the pleasure of playing with him at great length in Joe Newman's Quintet. We played at Count Basie's club many times, uptown in New York City, and at other jobs, and he was a wonderful player. He preferred to play tenor on those jazz jobs, even though he was equally adept on alto. We lost Oliver much too soon; he died at age forty-three after he moved to California. While he was in New York City, I had the pleasure of making five different albums with him. Among the most outstanding—according to him, as well as most people—were *Afro-American Sketches* and *Jazzhattan Suite*, which I did with him; it was actually made under the name *Jazz Interactions Orchestra*. He did a lot of other writing, of course, and did other albums I played on.

He got a lot of social static for using Phil Woods and me and a few other white players on his record dates, which made him very sad. He got in a lot of trouble for it. He cried in front of me when telling me how pictures of slave ships were put under his door, along with various bad messages about using white players, asking how he could be so disloyal to his own race. He said to me, with tears running down his face, "Eddie, I just hire people whose playing helps my music. That's what I do it for." It really hurt him a great deal. He was such a wonderful guy and very color blind. He was very down-home and as rootsy as anybody could be, but he also had a very non-prejudicial attitude toward using the musicians whom he felt could play his music the best. Among them was my dear old friend, Snooky Young, the great lead and jazz trumpet player from the Tonight Show.

Oliver's writing, I felt, had enough importance and value that I think he would have been a very logical successor to Duke Ellington, if he hadn't passed away at a young age. He had great color in his writing, an individual style, and great technique in his scoring.

On top of all that, he was a remarkably fine fellow. He and his family came up to my house a few times. We were good, close friends. I loved his wife and kids. I have tried to stay in touch with Oliver Nelson Jr., who is a very, very fine flautist in the Midwest. We've talked on the phone a few times, and I went out to do a tribute to his dad in St. Louis, which was his hometown. It was nice to work with Oliver Nelson Jr. He played great—he's a great guy and in the same tradition as his dad. I felt that it would be remiss in this book to not give due credit to Oliver Nelson, a very brave soul, a very talented and gifted man, whom we lost much too early.

THE NEWER STUFF

The late '40s, '50s, and '60s were some of the most adventurous times in music, with new composers and new music. I was lucky enough to be involved with a great deal of it, like when Gerry Mulligan came to the forefront, as well as Gil Evans, Teddy Charles, and Teo Macero. They were new, fine composers and made some great music. I don't think there has been a period any richer. I was so fortunate to have been around New York at the time. I didn't spend too many years on the road, because after Charlie Ventura, my mother got sick and I thought I should stay home for a while.

BALANCHINE, STRAVINSKY, & BERNSTEIN

Working with George Balanchine was one of the two biggest thrills of my life, outside of the jazz idiom. I was hired to work with him when he was performing with the New York City Ballet when he tried some jazz scores. I actually got to sit down and talk with him for fifteen minutes. I love the ballet. My wife and I always had season ballet tickets. I asked him, "Maestro, these complex moves—are they all sketched out on paper?"

He said, "No, my boy," and he pointed to his head.

"In other words, every move in every ballet of yours is all here?" I asked, pointing my head.

"They're all here."

I said, "Thank you. I've been wanting to ask that question."

He said, "There are some choreographers that do sketches. They do a lot of notes and that's fine. But I never have."

"It sounds to me like when you create something, it's so different that it stays with you."

"That's exactly right," he said. "I try not to repeat myself."

I don't remember what score it was that had the jazz stuff that I played on, but later on, he told the New York Times, "Shaughnessy has a beat like steel," and I was ready to go to heaven. George Balanchine was one of my idols—along with Stravinsky and Leonard Bernstein.

I did have the chance to open the door once for Mr. Stravinsky. During the '60s, I did a lot of recording at Columbia at 30th Street and 3rd Avenue. I was coming in to do a record date, and walking toward me in the hall of the first floor was Igor Stravinsky, carrying a big score in his arm. I held the door open for him and said, "Maestro, a pleasure." And he said, "Thank you, my boy." I don't think he was even five feet tall, and he had a great big hawk nose—the perfect sketch subject. I walked on clouds all day.

Dizzy Gillespie and Charlie Parker had said, "You gotta listen to Igor Stravinsky because he changes rhythm so much." I listened to all of his music.

Teo Macero, a wonderful composer and fine saxophonist, later became famous as the producer for Miles Davis. He had a long history before that as

Big Sid Catlett– My first idol and mentor

First teacher Bill West and his wife, New York City 1982

Godson Bob Moses & Ed

Moe Goldenberg, teacher & friend

1948: "3 Dueces" Club on 52nd St. Sitting in with Chas Ventura Bill Harris Group on Dave Tough's drums

1948: With Kenny O'Brien (bass) playing with Charlie Ventura in Detroit: first national recognition

First free drum set! With Charlie Ventura Band, Chicago

Playing the Newport Jazz Festival in 1955 with Jerry Mulligan

Capitol Theater with Frank De Vol Band (4 shows per day) 1958

My friend, Buddy Rich.
"Of course, I'm the best!"

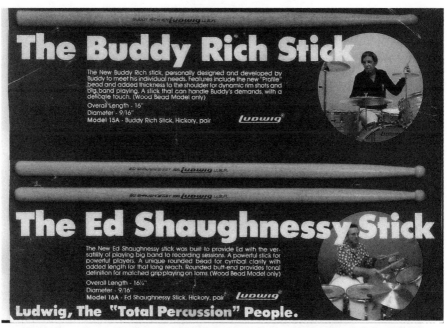

"I was very proud when Ludwig introduced my signature stick in 1976!"

Ludwig has always been great to work with, both under William F. Ludwig and through Jim Catalano in the Conn-Selmer era since they bought Ludwig in 1981. I have also enjoyed great endorsement relationships with Sabian cymbals and Pro-Mark drum sticks.

Doc's band showing our Grammy
awards for
"Tonight Show Band Volume 1"

On the road with Doc Severinsen

White House Correspondent's Dinner, 1961
(l-r) President Kennedy, Benny Goodman, Teddy Wilson, Ed Shaughnessy,
George Duvivier, Road Manager

To Ed
with admiration
& affection
Johnny Carson

"Doc" Severinsen Band with Johnny, Johnny Carson's last week, May, 1992

Ed organized this reunion in June of 2007, 15 years after Johnny Carson retired

**Ed receiving the Percussive Arts Society's Hall of Fame award from PAS
Executive Director Steve Beck, November, 2004**

Ilene Woods

Dan's family with Ilene, 2005
Dan, Nicah, Amarah

1983
Two handsome guys!
Dan   Jim

Ilene, Jim, & Dan
1972: First year in California

PAYING IT FORWARD

Ever mindful of all the talented yet patient and kind teachers and performers who took the time to help him along, Ed early on joined the ranks of teachers with real missions. He has not limited his educational contributions to private lessons and clinics, but has made it possible for many students to study with a variety of instructors. Ed has sponsored scholarships at North Texas State (5 years,) Kansas State University (4 years,) and the Skidmore Jazz Institute (8 years.) The first recipient of a North Texas State scholarship was Steve Houghton, a past president of the Percussive Arts Society. Ed volunteers at four local high schools as a drum set coach. "I very much enjoy the kit coaching," says Ed, "because I can reach more than one young drummer at a time. Teaching is so rewarding in it's own way."

Ed recently created the "Cinderella" award for a promising young singer in memory of his beloved late wife Ilene.

Ed with Maddie Petersil at the 2011 L.A. Jazz Society 28th annual awards dinner hosted by Leonard Maltin. Ed presented promising young singer Maddie with a cash prize, The Cinderella Award in honor of Ilene.
(photo by William Kidston)

With Jack Dejohnette

**With Bill Ludwig II,
at 1980 NAMM Convention**

**Cinncinatti Symphony on PBS, 1986
(l-r) Gerry Mulligan, Ed Shaughnessy, Doc Severinsen, Eric Kunzel, Buddy Mor-
row, Eddie Daniels, Dave Brubeck, Ray Brown**

Louie Bellson, Ed, and some of their fans, 1996 NAMM

82nd Birthday Bash with my
band January 29, 2011

Ed with the 250-member University of Wisconsin band, April, 2011

Performing with my "discovery" Diane Schuur at the Playboy Festival, June, 2009, Warner Park, California

With Diana Schuur at the Playboy Festical in June, 2009. I found her in 1975 in Puyallup, Washington.

**Ed & Louis Bellson on a clinic tour in Connecticut, 1998
("My mentor– outplayed me easily!")**

Playboy Festival, June 2009

a composer—and very rightfully so. He wrote a piece on request by Leonard Bernstein called "Fusion" for the New York Philharmonic at Carnegie Hall. Leonard Bernstein said, "I want to bring in a good jazz group of six or seven guys, put them in the middle of the Philharmonic, and we'll all play together," and that's what Teo did. He wrote the piece, and I so enjoyed working with Lenny. He had all that charisma everyone talked about.

I think Gustavo Dudamel, the music director of the Los Angeles Philharmonic, is the first guy to come along to have Bernstein's kind of charisma. It goes beyond technique. There are a million good conductors, but the joy and passion Gustavo emanates for the music is wonderful. Lenny was sometimes criticized for being showboaty, and some might say that about Gustavo also, but he's not. It's the passion for the music.

Working with Lenny was just great. I remember we were waiting to go out to play the concert, and he said to me, "Eddie, let's go out and swing like hell." I thought, "Isn't that great for the great symphonic conductor to say that?"

We had a good performance. That was the only time I worked with him, but it did require at least three rehearsals, and it was such a thrill. When you idolize someone so much, even something like just opening the door, as I did for Stravinsky, is such a meaningful moment.

THE SIXTIES

I was fortunate to make five albums with Count Basie, which thrilled me to no end. Two of my favorite bands were Basie's and Woody Herman's. To me, they had the best rhythmic feel; it was the most infectious. Basie had that blues-oriented groove. Duke's band had brilliant writing and brilliant music, but it didn't have that type of groove. It had its own type, just like Benny Goodman had its own type of swing.

I had never played with Basie, but I got a call from Teddy Reig, who was managing Count Basie, and he said, "Sonny Payne can't make these couple of record albums, and we'd like you to come and do it."

I said, "I'll have to get off the Tonight Show, but I think Doc will let me off for Count Basie." which he did. We recorded the first album, called Broadway Basie's Way, which was a lot of Broadway tunes arranged for Basie's band. I enjoyed the hell out of it. After the first date was over, he walked over to me and said, "Hey, Shaun, you fit the band like a glove. We're gonna have a great time." I walked home feeling ten feet high. I felt like I would know how to play for him, like a lot of other things.

As I said, I wouldn't play for Benny Goodman the way I played for Charlie Parker. If I have any strength, it's my versatility. I'm not the world's most original or style-setting drummer, but I'm versatile. I sound like myself, I'm glad to say, because I never tried to imitate another drummer, even when I was sixteen. I had heard from all the great drummers that you must be yourself, and with Basie, I didn't have to change my style. I had a style that fit, and I think he knew that.

I had worked with a couple of guys in the band, like Eddie "Lockjaw" Davis, who was the main soloist. I'm sure he said to Basie, "I've worked with him, and I know he'll fit in." The dates went flawlessly, and not only did Basie complement me, but Freddie Green, the historic guitarist, came up to me after that first date and said, "I'd like you to know I'm bringing my best guitar tomorrow."

I said, "That sounds nice, Freddie. What is that about?"

And he said, "I'm bringing my best guitar because the feel is so good. I don't bring my best guitar unless the feel is really good. I don't take it out of the house very much." I walked home on cloud nine. I thought, "I can die and go to heaven now!"

Two months later, we made Hollywood Basie's Way, where they recorded all Hollywood songs. Historically, Hollywood Basie's Way was the only time Roy Eldridge, the famous trumpet player who was with Basie at that time, played a solo number, "Here's That Rainy Day." History buffs must have that record. Out of the five I made, those were the two best.

DON ELLIS (Early '60s)

When I was about sixteen years old, I went to a concert of Indian dancing (from India). As much as I enjoyed the dancing, I was fascinating by the accompaniment by a few tabla players. Tabla is a pair of Indian drums, played by sitting cross-legged on the floor. Even though I had only been a drummer for two years, I could tell they were playing things that were far advanced, rhythmically, from anything we did in American jazz drumming. I kind of tucked that away in my head to learn about sometime in the future.

So another fifteen years passed, and I ended up knowing a great California trumpet player and composer named Don Ellis. He was very much in the far future of odd times, having a band play in 23/4 and 19/8. I heard some of his music on record, and he had this enormously complex bunch of music played by a twenty-one piece band. I thought it was great when I heard it on record originally, and then I heard it in person. He and I became friends, and then I interviewed him for a now defunct magazine called Jazz. In the course of our friendship, I said that I would love to study tabla, and he said, "I could hook you up with Alla Rakha, the world's greatest tabla player. He plays with Ravi Shankar, and they're all very good friends of mine."

"I didn't know that," I said, "otherwise I would have haunted you and asked you for this."

"Let me make a call or two," he told me, and the next day he said, "Here's Alla Rakha's number. You can arrange a lesson with him right away."

It was like a miracle to me because at that time in the '60s, no one was teaching tabla in New York—not that I knew of, anyway. So I started studies with Alla Rakha, and I continued for about three years. He was based in New

York in an apartment because at that time, he and Ravi and another player would go out and play concerts around the country and then come back to New York. I was very lucky, in a way, that he was staying in New York part of the time, instead of going all the way back to India. Lessons with Alla Rakha were a joy. He was a fun man, a happy man, and so brilliant on those drums that I can't even describe it. I can't put into words the sound that he got out of those two drums with just his fingers and his hands, but it would be equal to saying, "Buddy Rich gets a great sound on the snare drum"—that was Alla Rakha on the tabla drums. He had a thing of teaching the old system: the guru/disciple, where he did not write anything down, but he would play something for me. If I said, "Could you play that?" He would play it ten times if I needed it. Usually, I would need it three or four times. He didn't mind if I brought a tape machine, a big pad and pencil, anything I wanted to do. I would tape the lessons and write things down so when I got back I wouldn't miss anything, because it is a rather complex form of drumming. He started me out rather simply, however, teaching me the syllables. I got a little bit into the world of Indian music. I not only studied with Alla Rakha and practiced the tabla a lot, but I went to some Indian concerts, and Alla Rakha would take me to some Indian parties, where there were some of the most exquisite, elegant, and refined women I have ever seen in my life. They wore very colorful saris. It was another world.

Alla Rakha would accompany a ballad on the tabla with soft sounds, and it was something I had never experienced with women singing. It was so melodic. It was the equivalent of what we do with brushes, but a helluva lot better, more melodic.

I said to him later, "Thank you. That was the most wonderful party. Aside from the gorgeous women, the way you played on the ballads ..."

He said, in his way, "If you can play the tabla well, there are ways of playing with soft music. It doesn't stick out; it accompanies."

They would have a sarod, which is a simple stringed instrument, and the tabla, and a beautiful girl would sing. I thought I was in heaven some-where. It was like taking a lesson with Alla Rakha.

As soon as I opened the apartment door in New York, I smelled the food cooking. He cooked his own Indian food, and he'd have some Indian music playing. It was like stepping into another world, and I'd sit and have a two-hour lesson, at the very least. Eventually, the light began to blink, and I started to understand, although it still only put me in the infancy of that drum-ming.

I had the good fortune of studying with Alla Rakha for three years before he went back to India. He would make food and tea, and a lesson that should have been an hour would sometimes turn into three hours. Historically, this was how it was with his teacher, too. He lived at his teacher's house when he was young, and he would sometimes drum twelve hours a day. If you talk about devotion, you have to look into the Indian tradition—that's devotion. He didn't think anything of it. He said, "Oh, we all did that." That's why they sound so great.

I also had the pleasure to get to know Ravi Shankar, who is a charming man and a great virtuoso on the sitar. I think he's about ninety now and still going strong. He has a talented daughter as well, and I've heard her play. I had the pleasure to make a record with Ravi Shankar and Alla Rakha and some other American jazz musicians. I was one of the drummers on *Shankar Family and Friends*, which George Harrison produced. That was a great thrill for me. This opened up a world to me.

I started using some of the rhythms on drum set, and then I went further and started doing an Indian tradition when I'd get a long drum solo at a festival or at Doc's shows—he'd always give me my own five or six minutes. I'd start singing some of this Indian stuff and playing the stuff I sang on the drums with my bare hands. Tabla players have done this for centuries, but I don't think any American drummer had done it before me, not that I know of. Today, Steve Smith is doing it, and that's great. He's gone deeper into the Indian rhythm thing now than even I did. He's a terrific guy who I admire a great, great deal. He's done so much to propagate the Indian rhythm thing. But to blow my own horn, I must say I started presenting Indian stuff at every clinic I did back in the '60s, and for forty years, I've been telling everyone to at least get to know some of the basics, and I'm proud of that. I'm probably the first drummer people saw back in the '60s and '70s doing that in clinics. I had sheets printed out with some basic tabla exercises that you could actually do on the drum set, without owning the tabla. Everybody loved it. Everybody loves it in the middle of the drum solo, too. It's a great crowd pleaser. I put the drum sticks down—or throw them away, if I'm ultra dramatic that night—and I start playing with the bare hands and start singing the rhythms. The people eat it up. I still enjoy pursuing the Indian rhythm studies that I do—all by myself, of course.

Alla Rakha has since passed, but I understand that he was very pleased that on my CD with my quintet, which was some years ago, I dedicated a drum solo part to him, called "For Alla G." He heard about and sent word through one of his students that came back to the U.S., who called me up and said, "Mr. Shaughnessy, Alla Rakha told me to tell you he was very honored that you dedicated a number to him." That pleased me, because he died within two years of that. He has a great son, of course, Zakir Hussain, who is equally as gifted as his father, and in a different way, he is more expansive. Alla Rakha was very traditional, but Zakir Hussain has played with John McLaughlin and Miles Davis and a lot of fine jazz people; he still today plays with a variety of artists. He's one of those guys who is a mile wide. If you want to hear brilliant tabla playing, you must listen to Zakir Hussain. He made some duets with his dad that are just killer, and I'm so glad they did that before the daddy passed away. I had nothing but joy with that association and basically, I have Don Ellis to thank for that. What a great, great favor that was to me. I am so sorry we lost Don Ellis at a young age. He would have continued to astound everyone.

His records today from the '60s sound as fresh as ever, and I still say no one has matched his ability to get a large band to play 19/4 and 21/4, and you name it.

WHY THE ODD?

Before Don Ellis, I was interesting in what Max Roach was doing, and of course then Brubeck came along. I was interested in a lot of ethnic music. I had collected records from Africa and India. I had taught myself to play those meters. That's why when I hooked up with Don Ellis, I could play them. And I subbed in his band, which was one of the hardest things I've ever done. I'd never played in 21/4. His drummer was Ralph Humphrey. Don won a Grammy for scoring a movie and his band was hired to play the Grammy party—it was hard. Ralph played that stuff inside and out. He was one of the very best in the country at it. There was a drummer who Don Ellis had at the very beginning in the late '50s in California by the name of Steve Bohannon, who was a gifted drummer and a very fine keyboard player. He was killed tragically in his twenties in an automobile accident. But boy, he made original records, and I want to tell you, he was amazing. The story was that Ellis said to him, "I've got a new piece for the band," and Steve said, "What's it in?" And Ellis said, "Nineteen."

Steve asked how it was divided. And Ellis said, "So and so and so," and Steve just sat down and played it. Ellis said, "Wow, I have a really good guy here." But he was killed way too young. And then Ellis got hold of Ralph Humphrey, who did a marvelous job with the band.

But I, on my own, was interested in odd times. I wrote *The New Time Signatures of Jazz Drumming* because there was no book out at the time. Then about six months after my book, Joe Morello came out with his very good book on odd times. He had a higher profile than I did, so naturally, his book sold better, but mine is still a good book. The reason I wrote that book was because there wasn't a single book out on how to play drum set in 5/4 or 7/4. Nothing. It was translated into a couple of different languages.

I was always nosey about odd times. Indian and African drumming had always fascinated me, because it was so different from our drumming, and that's why I pursued the tabla. It's not so much that I ever wanted to become a real good tabla player, because I'd have to devote my life to it, but in studying the tabla, I got more into the rhythms. Coincidentally, in the early '60s, when I was studying with Alla Rakha and really only playing fair as a new student, I started getting calls to play tabla on record dates, because nobody in New York was playing tabla. It was mostly folk singers and rock 'n' rollers who wanted to add that sound to their music who hired me. I would forever tell them, "Look, man, I'm not that great a tabla player," and they would say, "We don't need a great tabla player. Can you make a pretty good tabla sound?" And I'd say, "Yes, I can, but don't expect the pyrotechnics of my teachers." They'd say, "We don't want that."

It would strike me so funny that I'd be sitting on a carpet in a recording studio, playing tabla, which was the farthest thing from my mind when I started tabla. I wasn't doing it for commercial purposes. It was completely the opposite. It was for intellectual interest. I don't mean I did a ton of work in the studios, but I probably appeared on ten albums or so, like Maria Muldaur and people like that.

THE SMOKIN' COMMERCIAL

I got a call from a contractor who gave me a lot of work, a guy named Marty Grupp. He was a great guy, a fine percussionist, and a very good businessman. He said, "I want you to come up tonight to Carnegie Recording at 7:00 on 57th Street and bring a couple of pairs of hand cymbals." I only owned one pair of hand cymbals, so I called the percussion rental place and told them to bring two other pair, which the contractor allowed me to do because no one had more than one pair of hand cymbals, or what are called piatti.

I went up there at 6:45– a good percussionist always gets there early– and there was no one in the studio. I looked in the control room and saw a couple of "suits"– people who look like typical agency men, which they were– the engineer and Marty Grupp, the contractor. Marty came out and said, "Ed, the cymbals that you ordered were delivered, and they're all set up on the stand. We'll be going in a few minutes."

I said, "Marty, what kind of weird date is this? I'm all alone in the studio? What is this all about?"

He looked around like it was some sort of CIA operation and said, "This is BBDO, the biggest agency in New York, and they have a new product coming out. They don't want word of their product getting out. That's why this is such a shut-down session."

I said, "But what are we doing for music? You have me and some cymbals?" He said, "It's not really music; it's more of a sound effect." "What is it you want me to do?" I asked.

He said, "Let me go back in the control room and tell you from there." When he went back into the control room, the producer from the agency said, "Take one pair of those cymbals, and see if you can make a dead choke sound with them."

I said, "In other words, you don't want them to ring like they do in the symphony?" "No, no, I want a dead choke sound." So I tried this three or four times, making sounds like chick, chuck, chook.

"That's not quite what we want. How about trying a different pair of those cymbals?"

I put down cymbal set #1, and picked up #2, and went chick, check, chook, cheek.

"No, that's not it either."

70

I said, "If you really want a muffled sound, do you want me to put a handkerchief in between the cymbals and then try it?"

"Oh, good, let's try that."

I tried that—but that wasn't it either.

"Try cymbal set #3."

I put up cymbal set #3 and went into my act of chick, check chook, chuck.

They all had that agency look of, "No, that's not it." And the producer said, "Well, I don't know what we're going to do."

By now, we had all been there for an hour and a half with my going chick, chuck, chook, chock, chack, and even though they were paying me double scale, I was getting very impatient out of frustration. So I said, "Look, you guys have some sort of secret thing going on, but in all honesty, you can't get the best out of me if you don't tell me what the hell it's all about. Maybe I can help you. That's what I'm here for—to do a good job. But if you keep me in the dark, I don't think we're going to get anywhere."

So the guy got on the mike and said, "Okay. In a week or two, we are going to debut the world's longest cigarette. We have an ad that we've already shot, where there's a cymbal player in a symphony in his tuxedo and tails. He picks up the cymbals, and he forgets he still has this cigarette in his mouth, and he catches the cigarette in between the cymbals because it's so long."

I said, "That sounds like a lot of fun." I reached in my pocket and took out a pack of long Parliament cigarettes, which were not as long as their cigarettes, but I put one in my mouth and said, "Roll the tape." I went up to the mike with a pair of cymbals and caught the cigarette between the edge of the cymbals. The first time I did it, they said, "Oh, man, that's it. That's great."

I gave them another six versions of the same thing, they thanked me profusely, and I left. I just thought how funny it was that all I did was the real thing, and we got the sound that fit the film. When I saw the commercial, it was as funny as hell.

WEARING A COUPLE OF HATS

While I was on staff at CBS they wanted me to do a weekend show where I would play drum set, timpani, and– as the added gimmick– a conga drum, which I could play reasonably well, for a gringo. They offered a good price for it, so I said sure, fine. I went for a Saturday rehearsal for a Sunday show. They told me I was going to play the conga drum on a stage with some sort of scenery for somebody who would be singing. And I would have to put on a Polynesian sarong. You can imagine how that went over with me! I didn't want to be unprofessional and quit, but I couldn't sit in a business suit if everybody else was in a sarong, so I agreed to it. Oh, God! I didn't have to wear it in the rehearsal, but when it came show time on Sunday, I went down to makeup and wardrobe, and they put a Polynesian sarong on me, along with and a crown of flowers on my head. I had to have bare feet. I had to run down from the second floor where the orchestra was stationed, sit down, and play the conga drum with my flowered headdress and Polynesian sarong. The fun part was that I then had five minutes to run upstairs to get ready to play an import symphony part on three timpani for the opening of the next act on the show. You can imagine, when I ran up there in my Polynesian sarong and a crown of flowers, what a thirty-piece orchestra did to me. I got more cat calls standing behind three timpani. And I finally ended up having to say to everybody, "Go screw yourselves! Go screw yourselves!" The conductor himself was in fit of laughter."

ILENE

Early in '63, my good friend Mundell Lowe called me up and said, "We're going to make any album with Ilene Woods."

I said, "Oh, that's the Ilene I worked with on the Garry Moore show."

He said, "She was asking about you."

By this time, I was divorced. When we had met before in the late '50s, she was divorced, but I was still married.

We recorded an album with Ilene for three days, and on the second day, after we got done, I said, "How would you like to have a bite of supper?"

She said, "That sounds great." I'll never forget—she always dressed with impeccable taste—she had on a cream-colored turtle neck and a brown skirt with brown shoes and a fuzzy-wuzzy jacket. I just thought she was the cutest thing; I really did. We went out and had supper. We went out a couple of times after that, and I told her I was very serious about her and said, "I can tell you're the kind of girl who doesn't feel like having sex with somebody without something else going on." And she said, "That's right." And I said, "Well, there's definitely something else going on."

And she said, "I thought there was, but I wanted to hear you say it." She was more of an old-fashioned girl. She had been married for seven years to an abusive husband, who also had abused her daughter. She had taken her daughter in a Volkswagen, driven to Florida, and divorced him. He got a clever New York lawyer and took everything from her, and he had been the money-maker in the family. He was so evil; he destroyed all her old pictures. She ended up trying to live off of fifty dollars and took a job as a school teacher. Even though she didn't have all her teaching credentials, they were desperate for teachers. She said things were so tough at that time that she and her daughter would catch fish for supper. Then she decided to come back to New York and get her career going again. She had an Arthur Godfrey job but quit because he never stopped making passes at her. He was notorious for that. He sexually harassed her, so she quit.

Ilene and I dated a few times, and I finally invited her up to my place.

We kissed and got warm and loving. She was down to her slip and said, "Are you happy now?"

And I said, "Now I have to figure this out: do you think I'm happy because you're down to your slip? No, I'm not happy now, but if that's all you want to do, okay."

She thought for a while, and then she said, "No, it's not," and that's the first night we made love.

I thought that was a funny story that we'd mention once in a while: "Are you happy now?" We proceeded to have a very loving relationship, and I don't think we were going out more than two months before I asked her to marry me.

Ilene's mother hadn't let her finish high school, because she took her to New York at sixteen, where Ilene got her own radio show on NBC. Imagine that—five nights a week with a huge orchestra, with arrangements written just for you. That's what the budget was in those days. She had worked with the biggest stars. She went on a "bond tour" with big MGM stars, where they sold war bonds to make money for WWII. During that tour in the '40s, she knocked on Marlene Dietrich's train compartment to tell her they were changing trains in an hour. Marlene opened the door, completely naked, and said, "Oh, I thought it was my producer."

That same day, Ethel Merman ran through the cars with the greatest big voice, yelling, "Get off the can! We're changing trains." Ilene said she was the dearest lady. On that tour were people like Lana Turner, who was beautiful but bitchy like hell, and Ingrid Bergman, who was more beautiful than anyone she had ever seen without a drop of makeup. Ilene said that Bergman had such a natural beauty, she'd come out in flat shoes, and the boys would go crazy.

But Lana Turner—if she didn't get a lot of applause from all of the crippled boys in the front row, she'd say, "What am I coming here and playing for a bunch of idiots like this?" One boy in a wheelchair heard her and said to Ilene, "I'll never watch a movie of hers again."

In 1947, Ilene started to work on Walt Disney's animated feature *Cinderella*. She was the voice of Cinderella and worked on it for close to two years. It was released in 1950. For all that work, she was paid $1,500. The story of how she got the job is quite fascinating. Walt Disney had listened to three hundred girls, but he hadn't heard what he wanted. Ilene had gone to California because of some very good offers from people like Jack Benny and Jack Carson. She got a call from a couple of songwriters she knew from the Brill Building in New York. They asked if she would make a demo tape for them, which she did. She made a tape of four songs and asked, "Who are these for?" They said, "These are for Walt Disney."

She really didn't flinch because she was used to celebrities. They took the tape to Walt Disney and played the first song, which was "A Dream Is a Wish Your Heart Makes," which is the most famous song from that movie. She sang it with that sweet voice of hers. Walt stopped it after the first song and said, "Who is that singing?"

And they said, "This is a friend of ours from New York, Ilene Woods. She's eighteen years old."

He said, "I've listened to three hundred girls, and that's the first time I've heard the sound. It's a pure sound. Is she a pure person?"

They said, "She's about as pure a person as we know."

Walt said, "There's something in that voice. There's an innocence and a sweetness."

And that is the way she was. He had his people call her, and she went in and spoke with him. He said, "Ilene, after hearing the way you sing and meeting you and seeing you, how would you like to be Cinderella?"

She later said that the thing she became most famous for—the voice of Cinderella—she hadn't even look for. She was just doing a friend a favor.

She proceeded to go to the studio on a lot of days. They drew Cinderella to look quite a bit like her. They weren't only interested in the facial look; they were interested in motion. They watched the way she scratched her head and moved her arms. When her father saw the movie, he said, "It's like I'm watching you on the screen." She said, "They watched me a lot."

Walt sent her a beautiful full-length mink coat for the winter, with a note saying, "I hope this will express some of my thanks," which was nice since she was only paid $1,500. At the end of the promo tour she did for the movie, a guy named Charlie Levy, who had a mistress, sent a guy up to get the coat. Ilene and her mother said, "Mr. Disney said this was Ilene's coat," and Charlie said, "Oh, no, you misunderstood Mr. Disney. That was just on loan." The next time she saw Walt, he said, "I hope you like the coat," but she was the type at the time who just couldn't say, "Charlie Levy stole it." A big executive like that had to be that cheap to take a coat off a kid. And it wasn't even for his wife.

Ilene and I got married on June 29, 1963, and she moved into my apartment. When I got divorced from my first wife, our deal was that I gave her anything I had in the way of money and stocks—I really didn't have a lot, but I wanted to keep the apartment, and she agreed to that. The apartment was on the tenth floor at 325 West End Avenue.

MILES DAVIS, A PLAYTEX GIRDLE, AND ABILENE CREAM

It was a great apartment at 75th and West End Avenue in New York City. It was eight rooms, and today it's worth something like four million dollars. It was on the top floor, overlooking the Hudson River. Around the corner, Miles Davis owned a brownstone. I had played with him a few times at jam sessions, and he seemed to like me. Funny story: in the 1960s I was walking up the street with my wife one day, and as we came around the corner, there was

Miles Davis, standing with a cane. I had heard he had been in a car accident, so I said, "Hey, Miles, how's your hip?"

"It's coming along," he answered. "Hey, Eddie, when my hip heals up, we got to go up and do some boxing."

"What do you mean, boxing? I only boxed a little in high school; I told you."

"It don't matter," he said. "It's good for ya. You lose some weight." Now this was a lot of conversation for Miles Davis, who wasn't very loquacious with a lot of people. He said, "Here's what we do. We each a buy Playtex girdle and get some Albolene cream. You rub on the cream and then put on the girdle, and then we'll box about ten rounds. We'll be sweating like two pigs, and that makes your gut get all slim and hard."

I said, "Miles, you're not even walking good right now."

He said, "I'll get better. We should do that, man. It'll be good for both of us."

I had never hung out with him socially, but for some reason, he thought this would be fun. I'll never forget it—it was so off the wall. My wife thought it was so funny. Imagine: Miles Davis, a Playtex girdle and Albolene cream.

A lot of celebrities lived nearby. I remember one time Gene Bertoncini, a wonderful young guitarist who was also an architect, visited our place and said, "This is like having a country home on top of a New York building," because my wife had decorated it in country style. It was really great. It was an amazing place. After a while, I would walk up four blocks to 79th Street, which was where I'd have the little boat that I bought. We'd get in the little boat and go up the Hudson River and out to Long Island. For city living, that was amazing. I'm not bragging, because I really wasn't rich, but I was making a good living. In those days, it didn't cost much to have an apartment. I used to think it was such fun for Ilene and me to go up to the boat, when there we were, in the middle of the city at 79th Street. Within twenty minutes, we'd be up the Hudson River or out to Long Island. I used to take all the kids of friends of mine out to the Statue of Liberty and drive around it in my boat. One of my best friends was Stan Free, a very fine pianist. He had a little daughter named Vicky, and I'd take her and my godson, Bobby Moses, out to the Statue of Liberty, and they thought that was so cool.

Ilene's daughter, Stephanie, was living at the time with her grandparents out on Long Island, because she was very interested in horses. She won the Madison Square Garden Riding Championship when she was sixteen, which was very prestigious. She didn't have a very expensive horse—hers was $5,000, and she was against $50,000 horses. Her horse's name was Trouble Maker—for a good reason. He didn't like strange people on his back, so other people had a tough time riding him. Right after she won Madison Square Garden, her granddad passed away, and then she lost all interest in horses because he was the guy who took care of the horses, the stable, and taught her to ride. The heart went out of her; she buried her big medal with him. We contacted the horse people, and they gave her another one. Today she lives with her family on Long Island and has two married children of her own.

Ilene had two miscarriages, and we started thinking that would be it for us; that we were going to have to adopt. And then all of a sudden, our son Jimmy was born in 1966. Two years after that, our son Danny was born, and we felt so blessed. Ilene said many times that there was no happier time of her life than when she was raising her two boys. I think that's why I married her. She was so different from most of the show business girls I met. She didn't have that inner drive for career only or career mostly. That was the only way she knew how to make money, because that's how her mother raised her, and she was talented.

She had perfect pitch, she sang in a sweet manner, and she was pretty, but quite frankly, unlike a lot of girls, she didn't have that inner drive. By then, New York was a little on the tumultuous side in the streets. Once we had had quiet streets, but the demographics had changed, and she could hardly walk the baby without getting a lot of cat calls. She liked to walk the baby from West End all the way over to Central Park, but it got to be uncomfortable. So in 1967, we went out looking and within two days, we found a small house in Port Washington, near the train station so I could commute. Quite frankly, we couldn't afford anything big. Even though it was wonderful living in New York for my work, it was a bad tradeoff for my wife. If the trains were running okay, I could get into the city in forty minutes, but the Long Island Railroad was notoriously on again/off again, so sometimes I'd drive. In rush hour, that could take two hours, even though we only lived twenty-eight miles away. I banded up with a few of the Tonight Show guys, and we would do the carpool thing, so each of us would only drive maybe once a week. We had a happy life out there. Port Washington is still a lovely suburb, and the little red house we first moved into was a lot of fun, but it was a little cramped, especially after our second guy came.

After two years in our little house, we found a much bigger house in Port Washington, a lovely home. It had a nice, flat backyard, whereas the first house had a less child-safe, slanty backyard. We lived very happily there for five years, until in '72, Johnny Carson moved the show to the West Coast. That was a hard house to leave. Ilene and I both loved it dearly. It was an old house, and I had a room downstairs where I could practice and play. The boys loved the schools in Port Washington, but work was drying up in New York. Rock 'n' roll was king, the recording industry was big in Europe, the jazz clubs were closing, and with Johnny, I had one of the few steady jobs left. All in all, it was a completely changed city for the musician. I knew I could make a living, but I thought I'd probably be sitting in a pit orchestra, playing eight shows a week, and I wouldn't see much of my family.

Raising the boys was the happiest time of our lives. We did lots of things together. Even when I couldn't afford it, I'd put it on the credit card and pay it off later. I was so glad I did. We took trips to Canada and to Monhegan

Island, which is out in the Atlantic, off the coast of Maine. It's sort of a "time stood still" place that I saw in a pamphlet. It was great. One of the most interesting things about it was that Thomas Edison's grandson lived there, but he used candlelight and oil lamps in his house—the inventor of the electric light's grandson didn't have electric lights in his house. Also on Monhegan Island was one of the great Wyeth painters.

The island had one big inn, one grocery store, one this, and one that, and the rest of the island was for nature and walking. It was just great. I read in the pamphlet, "Do you want to get away from it all?" We'd take a boat, which took forty minutes to go from the coast of Maine to the island. The boys just loved it. We could catch a fish off of any side of the island. It was one of those simple vacations that were so wonderful. I can honestly say that the simpler vacations were the best, like going to Canada, where there was no television or telephone in the cabins. We brought games along and lived in one big room with little alcoves for sleeping and did everything together. As soon as we got home, and each boy went to his room and turned on the TV. I looked at my wife and said, "I don't like this."

1963—THE BEGINNINGS OF THE TONIGHT SHOW

The Tonight Show had already started—not with me but with Bobby Rosengarden, but he was so busy doing so many other things that he didn't want to just do the Tonight Show. He was playing, contracting, and writing. He was very good at everything. He could play drum set, vibes, and everything. He was a little aggressive but a good musician. And then the other drummer had to move out to the West Coast because his wife had a health problem, so the show needed another drummer. I did a sub date or two up there, not with the band, but I played with Joe Bushkin. When the job opened up and they called me, I said I didn't want to take it. "I just quit CBS about four years ago because I didn't like a staff job," I told them. "It pins me down too much. I like to be freelance and work jazz clubs at night."

"That's okay. We only want you to work a couple of days a week. You can split it with Bob Rosengarden, and you guys can cooperate on which days."

First I said I wasn't interested, but then they said, "Can't you help us out? The other guy has to leave because of his wife, and Skitch Henderson [the bandleader] would really like you to sub."

I said, "Okay, I'll do two weeks for you while you look for somebody." So that was the deal. I got up there and started playing with the band. Sitting next to me was one of my good friends Clark Terry, and sitting next to him was another friend, Snooky Young. There were all these wonderful players, and the band sounded so good that I went home and said to my wife, "You know, honey, this is really a fun job." And she said, "Well, why don't you take it?" And I said, "I think I will."

It was the quality of the music. So I went to the contractor, Aaron Levine, asking if he'd called anybody for the job. When he asked why, I said, "I'm a little embarrassed to tell you, but to be honest with you, I've only played with the band three or four nights, but I just love the band so much that I'd like to take the job."

He said, "I never picked up the phone."

I said, "You're that smart?"

"Yeah, I'm that smart."

Skitch Henderson had hired the best musicians anyone could hire in New York. Tommy Newsom was the lead sax, and there were all these fine guys. So I took the job. Little did I think it would last for twenty-nine years.

HERE'S JOHNNY

Johnny Carson, off stage, was rather shy. It probably wasn't until about a week after I was on the job that he came up and shook my hand and said, "Ed, nice having you with us." I said, "Thanks, Johnny. It's a great pleasure."

When we lost our son Jimmy in 1984, Johnny called us and sent a beautiful letter. "If there's anything I can do … I'm so sorry." He was so kind.

About a month after Jimmy's passing, we went to see Buddy Rich play. Johnny was there, and he came up behind Ilene and put his hands on her shoulders. He said, "I'm glad to see you guys out." She never forgot that. She said there was something about the way he touched her shoulders that said more than any words could say.

About a year after Jimmy died, Johnny called me down to his office. I couldn't figure out what the hell it might be about. I went in and said, "Hi, John, what can I do for you?"

He said, "I hope I can do something for you. I have a bunch of snap-shots here that were mailed to me of your late son Jimmy at a party with some of his high school friends. For some reason, they were afraid to mail them to your house directly. They thought maybe I could give them to you."

I said, "That would be lovely."

"I know that might seem funny, but I guess they felt funny mailing them to your home," he said, "that maybe it would bring up bad memories."

I said, "No, look, he was having fun with his friends."

Johnny said, "I felt I should give them to you." He was very good in those kinds of situations. A lot of people said he played his feelings close to his vest, and I think he did. He told me that most of the time when he went to parties, he sat in a corner. He said, "I'm not good at parties at all." He was a little defensive, I think, because everybody wanted something from him. I saw it once when we went out to Ohio to do a big theater. The only place to stay that was close to the theater was a pretty nice motel, not a big fancy hotel, which was farther away. Johnny said, "I'd rather stay [at the motel] because it's only ten minutes to the theater." He walked outside one day, smoking, and some people came along. I watched him—he must have spent twenty minutes with these people, signing things and talking, and he wasn't grandly aloof. He got a lot of bad press for being cold and detached, but he did resent intrusion when it shouldn't be there. I think he built a little wall around himself. But I always felt that he was the kind of guy, in a pinch, who would come through for you, as I saw when we lost our son. The terrible thing was that a few years later, he lost his own son. And that was just after they had, more or less, patched up a spotty relationship. I felt so terrible for him.

He was a great guy to work for, though. I always say it comes down from the top—the good or the bad—and he knew how to assign responsibility. He would get the best bandleader, who wouldn't allow a wrong note to be played; he'd get the best lighting man; everything the best so it would be the best production. I only saw his temper once. They gave him a broken microphone two days in a row, and when he started rehearsing, the mike went in and out, in and out. He dropped it on the floor and said, "Hey, guys, you get me a new mike, or we don't rehearse." And boy, he had a new mike in about two minutes. And he was right. They had tried to tighten a screw instead of getting him a new mike. I also really respected him for being a guy who didn't bring his troubles to the job. He was divorced several times, but he never brought that to work with him, and that's why he was an easy man to work with. You never had to ride his emotional roller coaster, like with many people.

I have to include a salute to Johnny Carson and a big thank-you for keeping the big band and loving the big band during his whole time on the air. I know for a fact that NBC approached him three or four times about cutting the band down to a smaller band, saving money, telling him he could make a few more bucks. And every time, his answer, in essence, was, "If the band goes, I go." That's all he had to say, because he certainly was the biggest moneymaker at NBC and that carried a lot of clout. He loved the band. He didn't just keep us there for that fine job for so long; he really loved the band.

I have recently looked at some clips of the show on YouTube because of the passing of my dear friend Snooky Young, and it reminded me not only of how great the band sounded but how enthusiastic Johnny was about the band, saying, "What a great sound," and "How I love that!" He did so much in a positive way for the band that when we went out on the road and did some tours during those years, we had a custom-made audience. I'm sure they liked the music, too, but the fact that Johnny was so warm and outgoing about the band and lent his endorsement, it gave us a built-in acceptance factor. We were all very grateful to him. He was a man who, in a way, kept the last of the big-band tradition alive in a medium that has changed a great deal, as does everything.

I'm sad that there isn't a chance for younger musicians to hear a really first-class big band like Doc Severinsen's big band on a regular basis. It's a great tradition and a great sound, so I hope they pursue other ways, like CDs and DVDs, to hear great big-band music played. I was so lucky to be in that job to play quality music with a great bandleader and great, great star who couldn't have appreciated his band any more than he did. He was a champ in every way.

Johnny was an amateur drummer, too. Once in a while he'd come into Eddie Condon's jazz club where I was playing, and I'd try to get him to play. Usually, he wouldn't, but he would once in a while. He'd have to have a few drinks. I was subbing for Cliff Leeman, the drummer, and he felt comfortable playing Dixieland music. He was comfortable playing the older style music as well. He wouldn't have gotten up at Birdland or somewhere like that. Buddy Rich could get him up once in a while. He'd say, "Well, I'm not going to play if you won't play a tune." I saw that happen once or twice. He was not the kind of guy who went out to play, though. He had to be dragged, kicking and screaming. He was fairly good for an amateur. He had a good sense of rhythm.

On the Tonight Show, we would get him up to play in earlier years once in a while. And then finally, he wouldn't do it anymore. Buddy Rich asked him once when he was a guest, "Why don't you ever play with the band anymore?"

And he said, "Because between you and Shaughnessy, I feel like a fool," which was sort of a compliment. But he liked to play, and he did play at home on a drum set Buddy Rich gave him. A former student of mine in New York, Don Sweeney, followed me out to California, and I got him the job as band librarian. His drums were stolen, and when Johnny heard that, he gave Don his drum set. So I ordered a drum set—a clone of the one Buddy had given him—for Johnny's Malibu house, and he asked me to come over and set it up for him.

Speaking of setting up drums, there was one time in the '80s when I came in to the *Tonight Show* when Buddy Rich was going to be a guest. I got there early, and when I walked in, the only person in the studio was Buddy, who was cursing at the top of his lungs: "God damn, son of a bitch, sending me this crap, this shitty drum set!"

I walked in and said, "Hey, hello to you, too. What's going on with you?"

"Look at this fucking thing Professional Drum Shop sent me." It was a beautiful, brand-new set of Ludwig drums.

I said, "What's going on?" He had the floor tom upside down and was trying to set it up, and when he tried to play it, it was very low because he had the legs on upside down. I said, "Is this what you're cursing about?"

He said, "This God damn thing—how can I play the floor tom? It's way down here."

I said, "You bonehead. You have the legs on upside down."

"No, I don't." "You do. Naturally, with the legs on upside down, the

80

drum can't come up any higher."

And then he said the classic line: "Well, shit, what you do want? I haven't set up drums in forty years."

I said, "All right, let's relax," and I turned the drum over and put the legs in right. It was so funny.

We used to have summer symposiums at universities, where guys like me would teach kids, and there would be a symphony playing. It was called the Ludwig Symposium, after Mr. Ludwig, who owned the Ludwig Drum Company. Mr. Ludwig once gave a big dinner down at a southern university after the symposium, and Buddy was the guest of honor, along with his band. I was sitting next to Buddy, eating dinner. Mr. Ludwig came in and said, "Oh, I'm sorry. I couldn't help it, but when you were rehearsing, I noticed that a wrinkle was in your front bass drum head. I had to fix it to make it look better."

Buddy said, "What? You did what?"

"I tightened the front head to get that wrinkle out of the front head," Mr. Ludwig repeated.

"You get your ass back in there and put the wrinkle back in the front head!" Buddy said. "That drum is sounding the way I want it. When you tighten the front head, you're changing the tone of it."

Mr. Ludwig put the wrinkle back in the front head, and then everything was okay. Naturally, Mr. Ludwig had wanted the head with that Ludwig logo to look nice, and so he'd taken the wrinkle out. I thought that was so funny.

CH-CH-CH-CH-CHANGES

The real ascendancy of rock 'n' roll was in the '60s—Bill Haley and the Comets and then the Beatles. I was saying to myself, "It doesn't have to be your favorite music or anything you like, but if you don't play it pretty well, you're going to be left in the dust," which some very good New York drummers were. They wouldn't touch rock 'n' roll. I went out and bought the kind of rock 'n' roll I really liked, which was James Brown, and Sly & the Family Stone, so it was enjoyable to practice with. It's more R&B [rhythm & blues], but a lot of it is even more sophisticated than straight-ahead rock. If you can play those two well, you can play pretty much everything else. That's why drummers today are still talking about the James Brown drum beats.

Probably around 1960 or '61, I saw the light—this was prior to the Tonight Show. You had to be blind not to see it coming, so one day a week, other than the day I would teach, I would sit in my teaching studio, which was over the Henry Adler Drum Store, for two hours, with earphones, and practice to those records. When I got the Tonight Show job, I upped that practice, because we were having a fair amount of rock acts on the show. I never had a rock act complain, and that's only because I worked at it. I'm not that gifted that I could just say, "Hey, I'll be a rock 'n' roll drummer," especially because I was a jazz drummer. I know that it's different.

Contrary to belief, not just anybody can play rock. Some rather well-known drummers were brought to colleges for symposiums but didn't bother bringing their own music. They'd say, "Oh, we'll play some of yours," so the band director would suggest, for variety, that they play a jazz piece and a rock piece. The director would say to me later that the drummer couldn't play the rock piece to save his life. The feel is completely different.

My students would laugh when they would hear me up in my studio, practicing rock. I'd open my door, and the sweat would be pouring down my face. I wasn't ashamed that I was practicing it. I came up known as a different type of drummer. But when there was a rock act on the Tonight Show, all that hard work paid off, because I could play it decently. I'm not saying I was ever a great rock 'n' roll drummer, but I was a good rock 'n' roll drummer. I played over six thousand shows with the Tonight Show, and a great many of them were rock shows. I never had one complaint. I sent some subs in, and although I won't mention names, with three I sent in, Doc yelled at me, saying, "They can't play the rock for shit." I thought everybody was playing catch-up like me.

I learned to get Nick Ceroli, who played everything well, and after Nick, God rest his soul, passed, I got Colin Bailey. When Colin left town, I got Jeff Hamilton. The only drummer I know who adapted himself to rock 'n' roll beautifully was Buddy Rich, but I do consider him at genius level. Some rock 'n' roll drummers say that Buddy was the best rock 'n' roll drummer that ever lived, because he could do anything he heard. All he had to do was hear the patterns these guys were playing, and he would play one better. And his style, which was a little short and clipped, as compared to Elvin Jones, whose rhythms were one the most legato and long, lent itself to rock 'n' roll. That's why Buddy was so successful playing rock 'n' roll with his band. He really owned it.

I remember Anita Baker sat down with Johnny Carson and said, "That drummer of yours, Shaughnessy, can really put his foot into it." The band teased me after that.

THE GOOD, THE BAD, AND THE UGLY

BB King was such fun. He rehearsed the way he performed. He never took 10 percent off, meaning rehearsal with BB was BB putting as much into it as he would on the performance, and I loved him for that. He was very appreciative of the band.

Tony Bennett was always a gracious man. Mel Torme was always a lot of fun to work with. He always wrote his own arrangement. Sammy Davis Jr. was always a joy. I admired him so much. Talk about a lot of talent in one package! Dizzy Gillespie, Lionel Hampton, and Stan Getz were on the show in the earlier years.

In the earlier years in California, we had some great jazz singers, but in later years, we didn't have them—the producers didn't think they were good for the audience. We had Sarah Vaughan, who was always a joy. I knew her for many years. We had Carmen McRae, with whom I had made an album, so we were friendly from years before. We had my old boss Peggy Lee; we had Ella Fitzgerald, with whom I had worked two weeks in New York, and we were very friendly. They were all such great ladies.

I remember once Cyndi Lauper came on with a backing track, but the machine broke so she couldn't perform—she could only talk to Johnny, and the band applauded. I don't mean that against Cyndi, but we didn't like the idea of her coming on with canned music, so it was "score one for live music."

Phil Collins always had me play with him. He never brought another drummer, and he's a good drummer. When he sang, he wanted me to play for him, which I thought was a nice compliment. The secretary came to me and said, "Phil Collins called up and asked who was playing drums today on the show." I said, "Ed Shaughnessy." And he said if it hadn't been me, Phil was going to bring a drummer.

Among the comics, George Gobel was hysterical because there was a bar backstage, and he always had a few pops before he came out. He had that little walk that we recognized, and we'd say, "Oh, George has had a few pops," and he was funny as hell. George was brought out on the night they had Bob Hope and Dean Martin. The two of them were breaking it up with laughter, and then they said, "And now … George Gobel."

Dean had come out in a tuxedo, and so had Bob Hope, but George came out in a simple suit. He looked at them and then said, "Have you ever felt like a pair of brown shoes at a wedding?" And the audience laughed so hard, as Dean Martin flicked cigarette ashes into George's drink, which George completely ignored.

Steve Martin made some appearances, and I'm pretty sure the Tonight Show helped his career a lot. He wore the arrow through his head, and he played the banjo. Roseanne Barr's career got a big kick from our show, too. She was hysterical when she was doing the "I'm a domestic goddess" routine. A lot of people got their big break from doing the show. Jerry Seinfeld got a lot of exposure from the show, too. Joan Rivers hosted the show. Johnny was really hurt when she got her own show and didn't tell him. He had to hear about it through the newswires. I heard from a friend of his later that it really hurt his feelings, because the reason she got her own show was because he had let her do his show. So the first person she should have called should have been Johnny. Instead, he heard about it on television. He never got over it.

MY JIMI HENDRIX EXPERIENCE

I think it was about '69 when Jimi Hendrix was scheduled to make his first appearance on the Tonight Show. Everyone was quite excited about that. In the morning, I got a call from the Tonight Show staff, saying, "Jimi Hendrix wants you to play with him." I wondered why—Jimi had a wonderful drummer named Mitch Mitchell, but I was told, "Mitch is sick; he's got food poisoning."

I said, "Well, I'd like to talk to Jimi Hendrix before we lock this in, all right?" Within an hour or so, the phone rang and I heard, "Hello, Ed, this is Jimi."

"Hello, Jimi. I'm happy to help you. I love what you do; I love what Mitch does, but I'm going to say this in advance. I certainly, generally, play a different style, even though I'm a good all-around drummer. I'm going to give you a 120 percent of the best that I got."

He said, "I know that, because I was down the other night to hear you play with Charlie Mingus at Birdland, and if you can play with that guy the way you played, you're gonna play fine for me."

I said, "Jimi, fine. I'll do my best."

The rehearsal was at 3:00 in the afternoon. I had an extra set of drums, and we were all ready to rehearse with Jimi. Before we played, Jimi said, "Hey, Ed, just play as loud as you can, and give me a lot of cymbals. I like a lot of cymbals."

I was up there, beating the crap out of my drums. I used my heaviest sticks, and I was playing my heart out. Jimi was happy. The engineers said to him, "Jimi, be careful of some of those effects you use, because they drain our electrical system." This was a major studio, but Jimi was so concert-oriented and knew how to blow the people away, that the engineers could see by his tuning up and playing a little bit that his equipment could do that.

He said, "Okay, I'll be careful."

The engineer said from the booth, "Jimi, you hit that pedal on your right once, and the lights flickered. Don't use it."

He said, "But that's my special effects pedal."

"Jimi, I can tell," the engineer said, "that gave us a problem."

We rehearsed some of his famous tunes, like "Fire," and "Lover Man." We had an hour and a half off, and I went to Doc and said, "I'm going to the producer to tell him that I'm not playing with Jimi Hendrix in a freakin' funeral suit." We wore dark blue suits with a dark tie on the show.

Doc said, "Don't go to the producer. Do what you want." So I took off my jacket and tie and rolled up my sleeves. I said, "That's the right way to play with Jimi Hendrix. Otherwise, it looks like Squaresville."

Doc was great about those kinds of things. It got to be show time, and I came down from the band on a commercial and went to the other set of drums on the stage to play with Jimi. Jimi was there in his snakeskin pants, and he had a real look in his eye. I don't know what he did between rehearsal and show—I'm not saying I have a clue—but Jimi was feeling good. He turned around and said, "Yeah!" And I said, "Yeah!" And we started up.

During the first tune, "Lover Man," he was getting more and more revved. And I thought, "I bet he's going to do it." And sure enough, he hit that special effects pedal on the right, and the whole place blew out! They stopped the show, and then they came out and took Jimi's pedal away. That was the first time in history that the Tonight Show stopped. They said, "Jimi, you have stopped the Tonight Show." They got a replacement cable, and twenty minutes later, Johnny started in again: "Here he is ... Jimi Hendrix."

Johnny was a great believer in keeping the medium live, even with mistakes. His theory was even if we got a blip or he said something wrong, he'd keep it in. And he wouldn't talk to any of the guests before the show because he wanted it to be spontaneous. But that one with Jimi Hendrix, he couldn't keep.

There were only two other times when the show stopped in my thirty years—once due to a camera going out, which only took a few minutes to fix, and another time, which I'll get to later. Afterwards, Jimi came up, gave me a hug and a kiss, and said, "Thanks a lot."

THE OTHER TIME THE SHOW STOPPED– EARLY '70S

If you look at anyone who was in the studio that day and say the word, "Calhoun," they'll wet their pants. Dennis Weaver, a wonderful actor and a great humanitarian, started thinking he should be a singer. He was going to sing a western song called "Calhoun" on the show, but he couldn't be there for rehearsal. His conductor, who played piano, was there, and he had the music. The Tonight Show producer, Freddie DeCordova, said, "Gee, I feel funny running this without Dennis," but his conductor said, "I know, but his plane is delayed. He'll be fine. Trust me—I work with him all the time."

Freddie—great producer—said, "All right. This is very unusual, but what can we do?"

So the guy sat down at the piano and explained, "On this tune, 'Calhoun,' I play this, and then Dennis sings 'Calhoun,' and we say, 'He was a man of the west,' and play simple accompaniment.'

We get to the show; Johnny starts the show. Dennis wasn't supposed to be on for half an hour, so he's back there, getting makeup. Johnny introduces him, "I'm so pleased. We had a little bit of a snafu with his plane coming in from New York, but we have a wonderful actor and friend of mine. He's going to come out and sing for the first time on television ... Dennis Weaver."

The curtain opens. Dennis comes out, smiling. The piano player plays the little intro, and Dennis sings the word "Calhoun" in three different keys—

he was way, way off. And the guy plays it again, and Dennis sings it in yet another different key. I think he was terribly nervous. The guy plays it again on the piano, and Dennis howls it again in yet another key.

Freddie DeCordova walks over to him and says, "Dennis, why don't we have you come through the curtain again and you just go over and sit with Johnny?"

And Dennis says in his Dennis Weaver twang, "Gee, I'm sorry. It went really good the last time." And that's what they did. We stopped the show, and he went back behind the curtain, and Johnny said, "And here he is ... Dennis Weaver." And Dennis came out—but no "Calhoun." And if you say that word to anyone in the band ...

NOT-SO-FUNNY JERRY LEWIS, RAY CHARLES AND WHITNEY HOUSTON

Ninety percent of the acts on the Tonight Show were good to get along with, and Doc was a good bandleader who knew just what to do with a bad arrangement to make it sound good. As a result, everything would go along pretty well. Lewis was a little tough to deal with once in a while, because he liked to come up and conduct the band. Once I was playing as he conducted some piece with really grandiose gestures. He said to me, "Shaughnessy, you're not following the rhythm I'm doing. What's the matter? Don't you like to play for Jews?"

I said, "Only on Tuesday and Thursday." It was Monday. The band completely broke up. And he shut up. Usually, you think of something clever to say a half an hour after the fact, but I got a good one in right away, and he got off my case.

But I would say that for the most part, people were on their best behavior when they came on the show. Of course, there was Ray Charles, which has been an oft-told story. He actually berated me on the air, which was terribly embarrassing. I was playing with a pair of brushes on a cymbal, which is about as loud as a mouse peeing. He said something like, "Drummer, you're not listening to my rhythm." He was playing a very slow, soft thing, and I was hardly doing anything.

I wondered if it had anything to do with the fact that before the show, his conductor, who was a friend of mine, insisted on taking me in to meet Ray Charles. I didn't particularly want to do it, but the conductor said I had to do it. He introduced us, saying, "Ray, this is my friend Ed Shaughnessy, the great jazz drummer," and Ray said, "Well, I don't want no jazz when I'm out there." He didn't ever want you to play ding, ding-a-ding. He just wanted straight ahead.

I said, "Well, fine, Ray." I wondered if that's what led to his comment. It was almost as if he was saying, "You may be a big jazz name, but I can take you down a peg." That had to be the most embarrassing professional moment I've ever had, and people mentioned it, even years later. What everyone doesn't know, though—unless they've read Ed McMahon's book—is that Johnny Carson went backstage and told Ray Charles that he owed me an apology. I don't ever remember Ray Charles apologizing to me, but he told Johnny Carson he would. Ed McMahon wrote in his book that Ray had apologized, but I think I'd remember that. Ray probably told Johnny he would apologize because he wanted to be back on the show. I never knew about any of it until I read about it in Ed's book.

There was also a very interesting time when Ray came on, and there was an arrangement that called for some trumpet soloing. After Snooky, one of the most respected jazz players in history, played some stuff during rehearsal, Ray Charles said, "Don't you think you could play that with a little more feeling, man?" Of course, Ray couldn't see who was playing it, but as soon as Snooky spoke back, and Ray could tell from his voice that he was an African American, Ray said, "Uh, that's okay, brother. You just do that, and that'll be fine." It was a telling moment, and we all laughed quietly. Snooky was so offended. If there's anything Snooky did, it was play with feeling. He could play four notes with feeling.

And finally, Ray came on the show, and he was on Doc's case, telling Doc he didn't do something right. As far as I know, this was the only time Doc ever went to the producer, but he went to Freddy De Cordova and said, "I'm not taking music lessons from Ray Charles. You tell him to bring a self-contained band from now on." And Freddy went along with it, because Doc never did things like that—he was the most helpful to the performer. He'd bend over backwards. He'd get Tommy Newsom to write a new arrangement if he had to. But this time, he drew a line in the sand, and we never played for Ray Charles again.

Whitney Houston was like a piece of ice. She wouldn't even look at the band when she rehearsed.

ED McMAHON, TOMMY NEWSOM, AND DOC

Ed McMahon   Ed was an affable fellow, though a little tight with the buck. He once gave everybody a bottle of wine that I found out later he had gotten for free. The quote I like to use is from Mrs. Snooky Young, a very classy and elegant lady named Dorothy, who said of Ed's wine, "I wouldn't cook with this shit." The year he gave us the wine, he gave everyone in the office a little plastic radio, and none of them worked.

One of my favorite Ed McMahon stories is about a friend of mine, a businessman, who was traveling on the day after Thanksgiving from New York to Los Angeles. He was sitting in first class, across the aisle from Ed

McMahon, who had just done the Thanksgiving day parade for NBC. Ed was drinking champagne, and they were serving him a really classy first-class dinner. My friend overheard the flight attendant say to him, "Mr. McMahon, do you mean you had to work on Thanksgiving, and you weren't home with your family? Gee, that's really tough."

And Ed looked up at her with his glass of champagne and said, "It's lonely at the top." That's one of my favorite lines. My friend said he almost spit out his food. But Ed was a good-natured fellow and certainly a good foil for Johnny. Johnny could tease him sometimes about having one too many, and they made a great team.

Tommy Newsom   Tommy had such a dry sense of humor. One night Tommy said to Johnny, "That's a nice suit," and Johnny said, "Thank you. It's Oleg Cassini." And then he looked at Tommy and asked, "Where did you get your suit?" And Tommy said, "In my closet this afternoon."

Doc Severinsen   Doc recently called me to say how he's enjoying his retirement in San Miguel de Allende, Mexico. He's playing three nights a week in a Mexican restaurant, with two or three brilliant Mexican musicians who play violin, accordion, and guitar, and he's having a ball. Doc is the type who, even though he's eighty-three, could never put the horn down. He'll have to play the trumpet until they close the lid. But he doesn't want to travel and do all that conducting of symphonies and everything anymore. He's retired from that, but he still comes up to the States and does a concert or two, so he's keeping his foot in the door. Doc is one of my oldest friends. He and I worked together for close to fifty years, because I started playing with him on record dates in the '50s and then, of course, in '63, I joined the Tonight Show, where he was the lead trumpet, and four years later he became the bandleader.

Doc is a superb musician, one of the most gifted, natural musicians I know, but he backs it up with intense practicing. I think you could compare him to any classical musician who practices at least a few hours every day. Ever since I've known him, he would consider anything less than two hours a day of practice not enough. He used to have a calendar in his office at the Tonight Show. He would put a check when he did two hours, and anything less, he would put an X. He wouldn't want to see many X's each week. This is one of the reasons he kept such a great trumpet technique. I do think he's a great natural musician and has perfect pitch, but at the same time, he backed it up with dedication. I admired the hell out of him for that, and so did everyone else who worked with him. He was the kind of guy who never asked more of someone than he did of himself. He was a fairly strict bandleader—and I mean strict in the sense that he wanted it good, not to suggest that he was mean. He just wanted it to be quality all the time. He said, "I want the last show to sound like the first show, with the same enthusiasm and musicianship." And he got that. The band never faltered or fell off, because first of all, Doc would never have put up with it. I used to say to people, "There's only one reason you will get fired, and that's if you don't put out. If you play and act like you don't care." Doc didn't fire anyone for that, though. He only fired one person because he was late three times in about a month.

The New York band was a terrific band, but the difference between the New York band and California band was that Doc didn't pick the New York band. He was in the New York band and then inherited it. When it came to moving to California, he could then pick anyone he wanted. Doc deserved to have a band he could pick. He took the band the way it was given to him for five years, as the leader in New York, so when we moved, it was his opportunity to have the people he really wanted. Only Snooky Young, Ross Tompkins, Don Ashworth, and I were asked to come to California, and of course, Tommy Newsom.

Another thing Doc was really good at was fixing a bad arrangement. I could never understand people bringing poor arrangements to the Tonight Show, but Doc could bring it to Tommy Newsom or John Bambridge (one of our sax players who was also a great arranger), or whoever was in the band that night, tell them his ideas, and have them scratch out some backgrounds. And he'd change the bad arrangement. Doc knew just what to do to get it to sound pretty good.

He came to me before we went to California and said, "Ed, I've got a problem." The show used to go to California with just Doc, and he'd use Louie Bellson's band. Because of that, he felt he owed Louie, big time. I understood that, especially because Louie was a friend of mine. Doc said to me, "Would you mind, for a while, splitting the show with Louie?"

So for a while Louie and I did three nights and two nights; two nights and three nights—50/50. After about a year I said to Doc, "You know I love Louie. He's a good friend of mine, and I understand you owe him, but I'm out here with a wife and two kids, and I either need full time Tonight Show, or I go back to New York."

He said, "That's okay. You deserve that by now, but you have to tell him." So I went to see Louie where he was playing a club called King Arthur's, which doesn't exist anymore, and I said, "Louie, I hope there won't be any hard feelings between us." He was very nice and said, "Oh, you should have had the job before this." I don't think he was thrilled, because he liked the publicity on the Tonight Show—there's nothing like being on television to help your other work—but he was okay about it, because he was a good friend. I told him he'd always have the first call for sub, which is what we did. It was kind of a sticky situation, but it had to be.

I had a big reputation in New York in the studios, but when I came out to California, I wasn't entrenched in the Hollywood recording scene. They had plenty of great players in L.A., and they weren't about to call Eddie. I got a few courtesy things from Pat Williams and a few guys, to let people see me. They gave me a gig or two to let people know I was out here, but they weren't about to let people go who were working with them. Somebody who used Shelly Manne for ten years wasn't going to let Shelly go so Ed could come in. But it worked out fine. I always maintained that the high quality of the band was due to Doc's wanting it very good all the time. I think we were very overlooked by the critical press. When I listen to the last two albums we made, *Once More ... with Feeling!* and *Swingin' the Blues*, and I'm proud of them. Quite frankly, I think they hold up against any albums made by anybody. But I think because we were a television band, people didn't pay attention. I think Doc made a mistake on the first two albums we made by playing hits by other bands, but on Once More ... with Feeling! and Swingin' the Blues, we played more original arrangements. I'm very proud of having worked with that band. My wife always said, "That band has such a great sound." Doc picked players who had a good sound and when you put them all together, the band had a great sound. One time there was a club called the Americana at 36th Street in New York, and the club owner told Basie that he wanted to book Basie and the Tonight Show band. And Basie said, "You want me to play against that band?" He loved our band. He told me that many times.

ROSS TOMPKINS—THE PHANTOM STRIKES AGAIN

His nickname was the Phantom because somehow, he would leave a job but you would never know when he left. Sometimes you never knew how he came, either. The setting was the Cincinnati Symphony. I was with Doc in the early '80s and very often, when Doc would go out on symphony jobs, where he conducted and played, he would take Ross and me, so the rhythm would be good. He would do some pieces that had jazz feeling in the symphony, and he'd have Ross, who was a marvelous pianist and who would play the right chords that you wouldn't expect a symphonic person to play.

Prior to the Cincinnati Symphony event, Ross had missed the plane from Kennedy, and he had missed one or two over the last couple of years, almost giving Doc ulcers, even though Ross had managed to get to the jobs. This story is almost impossible to believe, but I was there, so I know it to be true. There was a terrible thunderstorm going from the East Coast across Ohio. All commercial planes had been canceled, and Doc was flipping because there was a person in the symphony who simply could not play the jazz pieces convincingly. Doc needed a real jazz pianist.

I was sort of doing the road managing, and he said to me, "Look, Ed, I don't care if Ross calls up and says whatever—he's done. This is it. I've heard every excuse in the book. He's fired, and that's going to be the Tonight Show and everything else."

I said, "Oh, Doc, how do you know he's not sick?" I liked Ross. He was a good fellow and a brilliant pianist. By the way, he didn't have a piano at home. He's the only pianist I've ever worked with who was really good and didn't have a piano at home. When I asked him about it, he said, "Why do I want to have a piano at home? I'm always working." He obviously wasn't the kind of guy who worried about practicing. He could take a symphonic piece and sight-read it. He did that once with Beverly Sills, and she looked at him as if to say, "What? You're in a big jazz band?" He probably could have put it in another key, too. He knew every song, dating back to when his dad was born, and he could play them in any key.

So Doc was growling, fit to be tied and listening to a lot of wrong piano playing in rehearsal. I said, "Doc, we'll get through it."

Doc kept saying, "He's done—don't forget—because I've heard every excuse in the world."

It was an 8:00 p.m. downbeat, and at about 7:40, the stage door opened and Ross Tompkins came walking in, wearing a tuxedo. I said to myself, "Oh, my God, how did he materialize?" I went over to him and said, "Ross, how did you get here?"

He said, "I rented a plane and flew myself out." He was a qualified pilot, and even though commercial flights were down, he was able to rent a small plane, and he flew himself to the Cincinnati airport.

I said, "Ross, I am so glad to see you, but your goose is cooked. I can't save your job. Your job is over."

He said, "No, it's not—wait until Doc hears what happened." We walked to Doc's dressing room, opened the door, and Ross said, "Doc, before you start up, you have to hear what happened." Doc was seething as he stared at Ross, but Ross said, "You know I was working at the Half Note last night with Alan 'Zoot' Sims?"

Doc said, "No, I wouldn't know that."

"Well, that's what I was doing. At the end of the night, the cops came in with a couple of detectives. One walked up to me and said I had to come down to the station with them. I said, 'Why? What have I done?' He said, 'A guy was just killed out on the street a few blocks from here, and he had your card in his pocket. You have to come down to the station.'" Ross's story was: "I had to go down to identify a dead body at the morgue."

And Doc absolutely broke up and said to me, "Well, I haven't heard that one." And he didn't fire Ross.

Ross said they'd kept him at the station for hours; he couldn't leave. But the fantastic part to me was that he rented a plane and flew out through a storm that had grounded the commercial airlines. Nothing was flying, but Ross was flying. He was an unusual guy.

SNOOKY YOUNG

Recently I attended the beautiful service for my friend of fifty years, Snooky Young, the iconic lead and jazz trumpeter, who in many ways was one of a kind. He was a great person and a fun friend, and we were quite close. I used to play in his little band in California. I loved taping him, which I did on three occasions, because he was a walking history book, very similar to my dear friend, Milt Hinton. I taped a lot of interesting stuff about Snooky and his family band when he was just a kid, and I can't tell you how much I miss him as a person, as a peerless lead trumpet player, and as a great jazz player and the master of the plunger mute. Nobody could play the plunger mute like Snooky. So we'll just say good-bye, God bless to Snooky. Thanks for a great friendship, for a very long time, and I'll be seein' ya.

MY SIGNATURE LAMBCHOPS

When Ilene and I got married, I had a full beard. I got tired of having a full beard, but when I started taking the beard off, I didn't feel like having a clean-shaven look, so I thought, "Why don't I leave something on? Why don't I leave these sideburns?" I kinda liked them and kept them. And then my wife said, "Don't ever shave them off, because nobody will know who you are."

THE MOVE

In 1972, we made the big move from New York, and my dear wife, God love her, packed up two boys, a Great Dane, and a whole house. My wife and I found a nice home in Tarzana with a beautiful pool for the kids, and a large backyard, and trees to climb, and we were very happy there. It was tough leaving, but we came to something very lovely. Plus, the weather all year-round was wonderful.

WORKING WITH THE MARSALIS FAMILY

About five years ago, Delfeayo Marsalis and Branford Marsalis called me up to come down to record with them in North Carolina. As we were recording, Branford and Delfeayo started having words—the two boys actually started going at it: "We go to letter B" "No, we should go to letter C"—they sounded like teenagers.

Then their father, the great piano player Ellis Marsalis, who was playing piano, said, "Okay, that's enough. We should go have some chicken." So we stopped and went to have dinner at the chicken place.

And Branford said to me, "I love the way you play, but you're such fun to work with because you're not afraid of black people."

I started to laugh and said, "What the hell are you talking about?"

He said, "I know so many white people who are afraid of black people. I sense it. I feel it."

I said, "Look at Joey Calderazzo, your piano player who has been with

92

you for ten years."

"I don't mean Joey," Brandon said, "and I don't mean a lot of the other cats, because a lot of the other cats have worked with black guys, and they're comfortable. But a lot of other white people are afraid of black people."

I said, "That's the funniest thing I've ever heard."

"Take my word for it," he said, "it's true. From the first time I met you, I knew you weren't afraid of black people."

I liked Branford from the first time I met him—he plays brilliantly all the time—and I think Delfeayo is an underrated jazz trombonist, arranger, and composer. I know Wynton Marsalis least of all, but I played with him once in Washington DC. Besides being a great musician, I think he's done so much for jazz education.

MY BIG BAND AND DIANE SCHUUR

When we moved to California, I did an occasional jazz job, but I felt that I wanted to do something else, other than just the show or an occasional club job. For the first time in my life, in 1974, I decided I wanted to get a big band together. So, the first thing I had to do was try to get hold of some good arrangements. I paid Bill Holman to write a couple of good originals. I didn't want to get a band that played everybody else's music. I got hold of a couple of other writers, like Hank Levy, who wrote for Don Ellis. I got Levy to write me a good 5/4 piece and another one, because I like the odd-tempo stuff. And I had a few other fine writers that became members of my band, like Ron King and Curt Berg, and we started to rehearse. I was very enthused. It was a great thing to put my energy into because I only spent from 3:15 to 6:30 at the Tonight Show, so I had extra energy to do other things. I always thought it would be fun to have a big band that would play some progressive music. With my high profile, I had no trouble filling Dante Club—I'm not giving credit to anything but the high profile. We would play Dante's and a few other clubs that could accommodate a big band.

Then, two years after I got the band together, they called me from the Monterey Jazz Festival and said that Woody Herman was ill and could I come up to take his place with my new band? I thought that was a wonderful break. John Lewis, who was the leader of the Modern Jazz Quartet, had heard from someone by word of mouth that I had a great new band, and I thought it was so nice of him to book us on word of mouth.

Six months before the Monterey call, I played a gig in Seattle, Washington, with Doc Severinsen. After our very successful concert, as usual, I was a little later than the other guys, wiping off and taking my time backstage. And a blind girl with big dark glasses sat down at the electric piano and started to play. I said, "Jesus Christ, who is that?" She was nineteen at the time. Then she started to croon the blues while she was playing, but not in a big show-off manner. She was with her brother, and she wanted to see Doc, say hello, and tell him she liked the music, so she was killing time.

She really knocked me out, so I walked up to her and said, "What's your name? I'm Ed, the drummer."

She said, "Oh, Ed, I so enjoyed you!" She was very spirited. "My name is Diane Schuur."

I said, "Where did you learn to sing like that?"

She said, "I used to sing at a black gospel church." She definitely had that flavor.

I said, "How would you like to come down to L.A. and sing with my band?"

And she said, "I'd like that a lot."

I offered to pay all her expenses and said that she and her brother could stay at my house.

She said, "Gee, that would be great." Then Doc came along, and she told him how much she liked the music. I got her phone number, and a week or two later, I called Diane and said, "How about if I book your flights for you now, kiddo, and I'll meet you at the airport?"

Six months earlier, I had commissioned Tommy Newsom to write a three-part gospel suite, starting out in a medium groove, then slow, and then up-tempo, with the idea that I was going to get a singer. So this had been very fortuitous. I had said to Diane, "By the way, I have this piece written, and you're going to sing in the second part of it, but there are no words," and she said, "Don't let that bother you. I make up my own lyrics." She was so courageous.

We had rehearsal, and the hairs stand up on my neck as I think about how the guys reacted. They were fairly blasé musicians—"seen it all, done it all" guys. I said to Diane, "Now, we're going to play the first part, and then when we hold the chord at the end, we'll start to play an intro—four bars, and then you do whatever you want." So we played the first part, and then we played the four bars intro.

"Oh, my Lord," she started out singing, like she had sung it twenty million times, "come to me." She was making up the lyrics, and the guys were taking the horns out of their mouths in awe—I swear to God. "Oh, dear God, oh come to me," she sang, making up these lyrics in perfect pitch, She sang with so much soul, and the guys were looking at me like, "Where did you find this girl?"

I'd never experienced anything like that in all my life. I was thrilled to death, because I had already spent $600 on plane tickets, and it was worth every penny! We got done with the slow part, and everyone started to applaud. We couldn't even play the fast part because everyone had put their horns down. She got tears in her eyes, and it was such a great time. Everything, I thought, was validated. I knew it in my heart, but really, here she was in front of a big band, making up lyrics in an arrangement she had never heard.

So we rehearsed our gospel suite, but we hadn't yet gotten the job for Monterey. Shortly after that, I got the call for Monterey, and everything came together. I was called the greatest talent scout in recent jazz history. She got more applause than anyone there. She did better than my band itself did. When she came out, Ilene was sitting in the audience, and there were three black women sitting next to her. Diane sang the first line, and the three women leapt to their feet and said, "God be saved." Ilene later said, "It was the wildest thing, Ed."

Earlier, I had said, "I'm going to bring a little lady out that none of you have ever heard." Ilene had bought Diane some new slacks, a little jacket, and a cute little blouse. She came out and sat down on a stool, and she began to sing like there was some kind of spirit in her. I'm not exaggerating when I say that when we finished the gospel suite, there were at least two to three minutes of a standing ovation—that's a long ovation. I also had her sing Duke's "Mood Indigo," which was absolutely out of this world. I've saved the newspapers that reported, "The hit of the weekend was Ed Shaughnessy's discovery, Diane Schuur."

My ego was gratified, of course, but the fact that I was right made me feel good for her, and I said this famously wrong statement: "The kid's future is insured."

But it took her ten years to get anywhere after that. All the magazines came up after that, and I thought her future was made. But the right agent wasn't there, the right manager wasn't there, and the right record company wasn't there. That kind of a debut usually gets you somewhere. She wanted me to be her manager, but I said to her, "Diane, I'm a player, not a business-man."

After that, she went back up to her hometown of Puyallup, and a ter-rible goniff (dishonest) woman got hold of her, and Diane ended up play-ing some dinky clubs. It was literally ten years later that she went back to Monterey, and Stan Getz was there. He took her to the White House, and Dave Grusin, who had his own record label, heard her, and she got her first record contract. I couldn't get her on the Tonight Show because the first thing they asked was, "Does she have a record label?" But ten years later, when they wanted her, she was too busy touring and working. During our time together, I brought her down to do a few other dates, like Dante's. I went a little broke doing it, but to tell you the truth, it was worth every penny. Once in a while, you have to put your money where your mouth is. I was sure that if I let enough people hear this kid, it was going to happen for her. I thought after Monterey, it was really going to happen, but it didn't. I learned a great lesson from all that—don't take anything for granted in this business.

My big band finally ran the gamut, because we didn't have any place to play in Los Angeles. All the clubs closed. But we had a great last hurrah. Mr. Ludwig called me up. I had only been with his company for a couple of years. This was around '79, and he said, "I want you to bring the big band to Chicago." He was the last of the classy family owners of a big company, and he wasn't afraid to spend a buck.

I said, "Whoa. Do you know what this is going to cost you?"

He said, "I don't care what it's going to cost. I've heard this big band of yours. I want you to come out to the big Chicago Music Convention (NAMM) and knock them on their ass." He paid for the entire band—sixteen pieces—and two roadies, hotel, food, and salaries … and we *did* knock them on their ass.

We did a few road jobs, but it was starting to be that time where it was getting to be prohibitively expensive. As we came to the end of the big-band thing, my accountant said to me, "Why don't you surprise me next year and try to break even?" I was actually losing money with the big band. I got great reviews with the big band—the L.A. Times gave us glowing reviews—but I pretty much gave up on the idea of the big band after a while, when the places began to dry up.

We never recorded, though, which was unfortunate. We had two record deals, but they went out of business before we had the chance to record. I started my quintet in the mid-'80s and had quite a bit of success with that.

MY QUINTET

I want to mention the two guys who have been with me for thirty-plus years: Tom Peterson, the great tenor player and arranger, and Bruce Paulson, the wonderful trombonist, who became famous at first with Buddy Rich and then wanted to work for a more kindly boss (a little humor there!) I couldn't have two finer guys as friends, as well as compatriots on the bandstand. They are loyal, great guys, with a terrific sense of humor. They both play up a storm, and I got very, very lucky, having them to work with through all these years.

I've had a pair of fine pianists through these years, too: Tom Ranier, the fine fellow from L.A., and an equally fine fellow, Rich Eames. They are both brilliant pianists.

And the wonderful bassist Jennifer Leitham, who at that time was John Leitham—I went through that change with her. I'm happy to say she's a happy lady today, playing up a storm of bass with her trio. And the other bassist who worked a great deal with us and is still currently one of the finest bassists in the country is Tom Warrington. So I've been very, very lucky, with all these wonderful musicians.

Since my friend Bruce moved to New Zealand with his lovely wife, Jan, I've recently done some work with Ira Nepus, who is a terrific trombonist. He's fun and a great guy also. I found out a long time ago, as a bandleader in the '70s, that a guy's personality is as equally as important as how well he plays, because the old adage of one rotten apple spoiling the bunch is very, very true.

I remember what Vince Lombardi once said: if you want to have a successful team, get rid of the whiners and complainers. I would like to say it works exactly that way for a band. Have guys with a good attitude and guys who are team players, and you will have a happy band. There was never any dissension in my band because the guys were great, and I tried to be fair. That's all a leader has to do for guys to enjoy working with him.

Thanks to all of those wonderful musicians for giving me a lot of years of pleasure. I hope we can keep doing it for quite a while to come.

TEAMWORK

It's like a great football team, running down the field, advancing together; or it's like a great basketball team, playing together, in that the team effort is the main thing. That's really what makes me happy—as well as many other guys I know—when I'm playing drums in a band like Basie or Doc Severinsen or Duke Ellington or any other fine, good band, and the band is really together and swinging, and you hope your contribution is helping a lot too.

It deserves to be mentioned that it's not ever a one-man show. I would even say that the enormously gifted Buddy Rich would never have had the value he did in jazz and music and big-band playing if he wasn't such a great ensemble player. Sure, he played brilliant solos—everybody who went to see him wanted to hear that brilliant solo he would play—but 99 percent of the time, he was playing for the band. And he played brilliantly for the band.

I think it's very important for everyone to remember that being a good team player is what makes you a good prize person. I mention this elsewhere in the book, and I don't want to beat it with a stick—no pun intended—but I just want to say that the idea of contributing, and the whole team feels together, and you're swinging together is just the greatest. Like any other aspect in life, really, working with others in a complementary fashion, in a helpful fashion, and in a democratic fashion is really what you're striving for. This is true even in a big band, where drums get a lot of attention. People say that the drummer is captain of the big-band ship, and my great, old friend Milt Hinton used to say, "You can't take it away from the drum chair." The drummer is the quarterback of the team, and like any other quarterback, you don't want to be throwing the ball away and doing stupid things. You want to be a good team player. That's what all the great quarterbacks were and hopefully, when you're a big-band drummer, that's what you're going to be. You're going to be a drummer who is a quarterback, playing for the team. And boy, when it comes off, there's no bigger thrill.

That's why, when Count Basie came up to me after the first recording date I did with him and said, "Shaun, you fit the band like a glove," I couldn't have been happier—except for marrying my wife and the birth of our sons, I don't think I was every happier. It was a great experience with Basie and Doc and the many other bands I've had the pleasure of playing with.

TEACHING

I'd been teaching in New York from about 1952, and after I had worked with Tommy Dorsey's band, I took a stand to stay in New York. I got a little studio over Henry Adler's drum studio on 46th Street, and I started teaching. I love teaching and really have enjoyed teaching for well over fifty years.

If you like to teach and, hopefully, are good at it, I think it's important to remember one thing: you can go out and play a great big solo featured number, like I have many times with Doc Severinsen and my own band, and you can get a lot of applause, and sometimes you can be extra hot and get a standing ovation (I've gotten those, and they're great), but no matter how great your standing ovation is that night, you have to go out the next night and do the same thing to get that reception. The applause or standing ovation is not a lasting thing. I like to think of teaching, though, as having a long note that just goes on into the future, without end. I still have students who correspond with me thirty or forty years after I've taught them. I'm happy to say that I can't think of one student who hasn't been working as a professional drummer since I saw that person as a student, which makes me feel good. They do have to do all the hard work. I just kinda show them how to do it. But I feel as a teacher, I've had a little bit of a piece of that help to them, and that's what is so gratifying as a teacher. The relationship with many guys lasts for a very long time, and that is so great. And I've also learned a lot when I teach. I come across exercises and disciplines that are good for me too, just like the student.

I've written two books, and put out a DVD of instruction on big-band drumming. Most recently, I put out a book on show drumming with a CD, with my good friend Clem DeRosa, a buddy of mine from way back in New York—a very fine drummer who then became a very fine conductor and probably one of the country's leading music educators.

The teaching has been very rewarding, and because I was interested in teaching and was reasonably good at it, I started getting quite a few clinics, especially once I got on the Tonight Show. Of course, my profile was quite a bit higher once I was on a television show like Johnny Carson's. But I still had to do a good job for the word to get around that I was a good clinician. The colleges and high schools throughout the country have to learn as much from the educational factor as they do from the playing of a concert with a band. I've done over six hundred appearances and have really enjoyed working with young bands and young people throughout the country.

Sometimes we have a great deal of fun in high schools. I've even done clinics with community bands, where everyone is there is a volunteer player. We have a lot of fun because people are there strictly because they like to play. It's the fireman, the judge, the local grocer, the butcher, the baker, and candlestick maker, and we have a lot of fun playing together. And I've had a chance, of course, to play with some crackerjack big bands in places like Notre Dame, Ohio State, University of Oklahoma, and so many great institutions. That's been a very, very rewarding sideline for me. I do the clinic in the afternoon, usually, and play a concert at night, with a morning rehearsal, of course. The way it works is I send my music out to them preferably a month beforehand, and by the time I get there, most of the directors have played those things enough so they sound quite good, and I can sit down and run through them once or so, and the performance comes off just fine. The school directors and bands take pains to make sure that it's going to be good by the time the guest artist comes, and I've always been very grateful to them for that.

I spent twenty happy summers as artistic director at Skidmore Jazz Institute, located at the fine campus of Skidmore College in Saratoga Springs, New York. We had wonderful students from all over the United States and other countries. From the start, Milt Hinton, the widely lauded bassist, was on staff and a total joy to play with. He was a fine teacher and historian for the students, with great stories of the early jazz years. We were good pals. My Skidmore period was 1987–2007, and I only stopped to be at home with Ilene when her illness advanced. During those teaching years, Ilene joined me at Skidmore and enjoyed it very much.

The idea of a clinic, of course, is a show-and-tell. I try to instill the discipline and behavior of a successful musician, and things like being on time, being sober, being respectful of people you work with, and being a good team player with a good attitude. These are important things; they really are. Sure, the nuts and the bolts of "Here's the best way to hold the sticks; here's the best way to play this beat" are important, but I think the other things are equally important—maybe more important, in a way. It's a common situation where talented players have an obnoxious personality, or a bad personal habit or behavior, or drug usage, and it just kills their career, even though they're gifted. We've heard that story too many times. I don't get up there and try to lecture or preach the gospel, but I try to throw in a few of these remarks and mention that a good, dependable person with a good attitude, who also plays well, is the kind of person the contractor or bandleader will call again and again. Those are the important factors in real life. That's what I've tried to instill in clinics.

Sometimes I've gotten clinics where I'm teaching to maybe a thousand people, if it's at a Percussive Arts convention (PASIC), and sometimes it might be just for fifty to a hundred people, if it's in a store or a small school. It doesn't matter. I do the best I can to get some drumming information and behavior information across. I'm happy to say I've been a successful clinician for a number of years, and what I like, especially, is that I get asked back to the same schools after maybe five years, and they have all new kids there. It's very nice to be able to go back and do a repeat performance. All in all, the teaching thing, which I'm still doing, is very rewarding. I rent a studio down at a place called Sound Street Studios. I still enjoy teaching today as much as I did when I first started—I really can say that—and I think I know a few more things now than I did then.

A PERSONAL HEARTACHE

Our son Jimmy was almost eighteen and excited about graduating high school. He and two other boys, who were long-time friends, wanted to go on a camping trip, which Jimmy had never done before. I was on a road trip for a week with Doc, so my poor wife had to make the decision. We talked on the phone, and I said, "Honey, of course we're going to let him go. He's going to be eighteen years of age. Where are they going?"

"They're going to Lake Havasu for a camping trip. A lot of teenagers are going up for a big get-together."

"Okay, that sounds fine," I said, even though they planned to drive all night, which I wasn't too crazy about.

On the 4th of April, 1984, as they were on their trip, some stoned-out serviceman came at them on the wrong side of the road at 100 miles an hour, killing himself and his girlfriend, Jimmy, and Jimmy's two friends. He took five lives that night. They said later he was loaded—I don't know if it was alcohol or drugs. Who knows? What's the difference? But they could tell he was going 100 miles an hour. And that's the way my poor son ended his life.

The policeman who sent word to us said, "I think your son had a head injury right away, and I don't think he suffered a lot. I hope that helps you. It looks like he had been sleeping, and the impact knocked him out." You always want to hear that. Whether it's true or not, you always want to believe that. We had him cremated up there, which is what he had always said he wanted.

My son Jimmy was an extremely bright boy and like a lot of bright kids, he was more bored with school than interested. He liked creative writing, which he did at home a lot. He wrote original stories, and they were all so interesting. Sometimes he would not do his homework for the longest time, but when finally the ax dropped, and his mom was called to the school to talk to his teachers because he was forty assignments behind, he would do them all in a three-day weekend. He was going to Pinecrest Private School at the time. We put the boys in private school because when we came out from the East Coast, the elementary schools were so far behind where they had been. Jimmy came home from school one day, and Ilene asked him, "Why do you come home from school so unhappy?" And he said, "Because they are playing Ring-Around-the-Rosie, and I want to spell hippopotamus." At six, his big ambition was to read the newspaper and understand it, and he did this by the time he was eight. He knew more about electricity by the time he was fourteen than I did. He fixed our front doorbell and made a few robots with mechanical moving parts.

He had infinite patience. He made stop-action movies with clay figures, taking one frame at a time. We thought he might be a budding Steven Spielberg; movies fascinated him so much. He collected movie posters. I thought if he didn't become a director, he would have become a screenwriter, because his imagination was off the charts. He was not athletically inclined.

He was a good swimmer, although Danny was an even better swimmer. Sports didn't really do it for him. I remember a funny situation where we bought him some stuff for football. He went out for the first practice and came back with some bangs and bruises, and he said, "Ya know, I don't think this is really my sport." We both broke up laughing, because I hadn't thought so to begin with.

His life was dominated by artistic things. He loved music, and his mom would say that during the day, she would hear everything from Yo-Yo Ma, who I introduced him to, to something from the Muppets, to a Doc Severinsen big-band album. He was very proud of me. Once in a while I took him to jobs. I was very proud that he was proud. We could really say that we knew he would succeed in some creative way. He could draw and sketch beautifully. I have some things of his up in the hall. He took after his mom in that way, who was, after all, a fine painter. I can't draw a dog; I'm lucky if I can make a circle.

Jimmy had such a big heart. He always took a dollar from his allowance and mailed it to the sea otter foundation, and he would always make a contribution to Save the Whales. His biggest heroes, more than filmmakers, were the Green Peace boat people who were trying to stop the whales from being killed. "I'd like to be on that boat," he would say. He was a born ecologist. I once dropped a little gum paper out of the car, and he scolded me so. I said, "It's only a little paper," and he said, "Yeah, but what if another 50,000 people dropped theirs?" And I've never done it since. He was concerned for the world. He knew about global warming way before I was aware of it.

He generally wasn't hard to handle. I think he and I had one or two arguments. Mostly, he did what he was told, but he was an independent spirit, and I had to go nose to nose with him once in a while. Neither one of my kids was a hard kid to raise. Jimmy, though, was the kind of a kid who wanted to do it his way. For instance, when I got him a motor scooter, I said, "You ride no one. You only ride yourself. You're not equipped to have a big load on the bike." It was a light bike. And I caught him with two kids riding behind him. I drove alongside of him, drove home, and looked at him. He gave me the keys, and he was grounded for two months. He never did it again. He had that little adventurous spirit that a lot of kids had.

He wasn't into drugs; neither of my kids was. I think they both tried pot—they both told me they tried it but didn't think it was too great. The bad thing about Jimmy was that he had a bit of a bully complex with his brother. I didn't find out until sometime after he passed on that he would twist his brother's finger or squeeze him and say, "You'd better not tell this!" And I'm sorry about that, because I only heard about it a couple of times. I did spank him because he had hit his brother. My credo was: "You hit him; I hit you." Keep your hands to yourself. But he did have a quiet bullying thing going on with his brother that I feel bad about.

But when Danny started to grow at sixteen, just before Jimmy passed on at eighteen, Danny was already taller, and Jimmy started to ease up. The

101

good part about this is that they started to really get along together about a year and a half before Jimmy passed on. That was what Ilene cried about the most. She said, "Oh, they were getting along the best, and they were talking about getting a little place at the beach together. 'We'll have chicks running in and out off the beach,' Jimmy would say, and Danny would say, 'Yeah, that sounds good.' They were getting along famously. They had passed that rough patch."

Boy, you have a quiet house after a boy like that leaves it, because you always knew he was here—there was always music or "Guess what I did?" He got a job at Fantasy Castle Store in Encino, and his job was to frame pictures and posters, which he loved, because he loved posters. One day Michael Jackson came in, and he had the chance to talk to him, and he was so thrilled! He loved that job.

Although the boys went to private school before high school, they did go to Calabasas High School, and it was a very good school—at the time, anyway. And the dean was very nice. Even though Jimmy passed away before graduation, the dean sent his diploma, which I thought was very kind. And all the graduation pictures had been taken. He was a very handsome boy. All the girls would palpitate for him. At Pinecrest, a math teacher, who liked him a lot but thought he was a trial because of the homework, told my wife, "One of the funniest things happened to me the other day with your son. A little girl from the lower grade was sitting on the floor, sobbing, and I went over to her and asked her what was wrong, and she said, 'Jimmy Shaughnessy talked to me.'" I thought that was such fun. One of his teenage friends said at the service we had for him that if a party was dying and Jimmy Shaughnessy came into the room, the party came alive. I thought that was a lovely compliment.

He left a big gap in our family for quite a while. My wife and I later wondered if we had paid enough attention to Danny during that time. We were so grief-stricken. I don't mean we fluffed Danny off—we would never do that—but we were grieving so. We brought it up to Danny in later years, and he said, 'No, Dad, I was grieving so much too. I don't feel you neglected me. I think we were all in such a state of grief." Danny is such a wonderful boy.

You expect to pre-decease your children, and it is so unbearable when it doesn't happen that way. The idea of one of your kids going before you—I felt like I was in a daze for a long time. After two weeks I went back to work, and someone asked, "Geez, do you feel you're ready to go back to work?" And I said, "Sitting around the house, crying every day, isn't good for my family or me."

I was much better going to work. When I did, Ilene would try to do things around the house. We tried to get some semblance of life back, because you have to. You can't sit home and cry. It was good to go back to work. It's a tragedy that has its own special circumstance became you're not mentally geared for such a thing. You're not mentally geared to lose your wife or your husband, but least of all are you mentally geared to lose your child.

A PERSONAL BATTLE

I was always an on-and-off-again drinker. I didn't drink regularly. I wouldn't drink sometimes for a week or two, and then sometimes I would drink too much after a job. I wouldn't drink on a job. I was never abusive. But what do they say? The ratio is ten out of ten sons or daughters of alcoholics flirt with that problem at times. I was never a drinker when I was young, which is funny, considering the world I worked in, where alcohol and drugs were prevalent. I think I started drinking on and off again when I was in the unhappy first marriage. But then you can ask, then why did I drink in the happy second marriage?

Around 1981, Ilene and I split up for a couple of years. She said she needed some time apart, so she rented a house in Carmel and moved up there with the boys, and I would fly up on Friday after the Tonight Show to see them. I started drinking more. I would come out of the Tonight Show and have a bottle of vodka in the car and start drinking. My problem got worse and finally, some friends of mine from the Tonight Show called Ilene and said, "You've got to come back. Ed is spiraling."

I always got to work on time; I was functioning, but the rest was bad. So in the spring of 1983, she came back, and we bought the house I'm living in now. I felt I had to make an effort to stop drinking, and I began to go to some AA meetings, which I felt were very helpful. Misery loves company, and a lot of good people go to those things. I don't think I really drank from then on. I was so happy to have my family back. I may have taken a drink or two when I went out of town, but not really around my family.

But when Jimmy was killed, I know that I took the hammer down and said that my family needed the very best of me, and I never took a drink from that day on. And that didn't take any strength at all. It took dedication and love for my family. You might think I would have wanted to drink because of the sadness, but what was foremost in my mind was that my wife and son needed me to be the strongest Ed Shaughnessy I'd ever been in my life, and I would be that for them. I've never taken a drink since then. I'm glad that I did the sobriety thing, because then everything, aside from Jimmy's being gone, was so much better. I thought, "Why didn't I seek this happiness before? Because I was too fucking dumb." I did it for my family.

It's funny—sometimes we do better things for other people than for ourselves. But as long as it's something good, who cares? Doing the wrong thing for the right reason, or the right thing for the wrong reason. Like what the shrink said: "The reason you went into the basement of the tenement and practiced the muffled drums for hours at a time was because you wanted to get away from what was going on upstairs with the drunken father. But that's what I call doing the right thing for the wrong reason. It drove you to the cellar, but you practiced more than some kids were practicing, and it paid off."

You get some great lines when you go to AA. I didn't go after Jimmy's death because I didn't need to—his death traumatized me off of alcohol for good—but one great line I learned was when a guy stood up and said, "I had one swell weekend," and you could tell he meant bad. He said, "I thought, 'I used to drink whiskey and vodka, so I'll just drink wine.' After I finished about a gallon, I was in the same place I was in with the whiskey and vodka."

The man running the meeting said, "You know what we call that? Changing seats on the *Titanic*."

Another great AA line was "Try not drinking for six months, and then at the end of that time, if you want us to refund your misery, you can always get it back."

But I want to emphasize that never, in thirty years, did I play the Tonight Show after having a drink. When everybody else went to bar or the cafeteria, I practiced. That's why a lot of people really didn't know I had a problem. The ones who called Ilene knew how miserable I was and knew how I was after the show. You cannot bring it to your workplace. There were plenty of guys in AA who went to their workplace bright eyed and bushy tailed, did their job, and went home and drank. That's not that uncommon.

I do remember one time I played after drinking, though, and I was just awful. I was in Vegas with Doc Severinsen. My agreement was that I could be home on Christmas Eve and Christmas Day, so I didn't have to go to Las Vegas. Doc said we could get one of my subs from the Tonight Show to play those days.

So I left home on Christmas Day, and I started drinking on the plane, because leaving my family at the holidays gave me such guilt. I drank too much, and by the time I got dressed for the job, I was half-loaded, and I played terrible; I know I did. Doc said I got by, but I think he was being rather kind. I remember I was in half of a daze. Doc said, "You got by; don't worry about it. I know you won't have another night like that. You never have." He was so gracious about it. He had known me, by then, for twenty years, and I had never done that. But I can remember that the boys had cried when I left that day, and I had felt so awful. Doc understood the problem because he had once had it and had given it up, so he was very compassionate.

When I stopped drinking, I can't tell you how many people were a little chilly toward me—former drinking buddies. They would keep pushing me to drink. But you have to find other people. You can't hang with people who are unhappy with you because you're not half-loaded. They're defending their own problem. There are a lot of nice, sober people out there.

ON THE COUCH

I went to eight years of therapy, which I first did because I was so unhappy in my first marriage. Of course, at the same time, once in a while I drank too much. The only problem was that I had a wonderful doctor in New York. He had a great reputation, with a great heart, and he wrote a couple of very good books, but the one thing he was not very hip to was alcohol. He said to me, after I had been seeing him for a while, "I think you could easily have a glass of wine or two with dinner." That's all a person who is prone to drink has to hear.

But he helped me in other ways. He helped me get strong enough to divorce my first wife. We were a bad fit. Therapy helped me get a better sense of myself, and it helped me to realize that if I knew I was unhappy with this woman after eight years of marriage, I had to do something about it. And I would drink sometimes because of that. We used to have group sessions, too. The first time I went to a group session, I already had a little bit of a reputation in New York as a drummer, and some people in the group knew it. They all kind of jumped on me and attacked me. They said, "You act like you have the world at your fingertips."

My therapist said to me later, "That's why I wanted you to come to group session. You don't act like there's a thing wrong in your life. There's plenty wrong in your life."

I said, "I don't lie." "It's what you project," he said. "You project equanimity. You have to talk about some of your problems in the next group session. Get down to earth. They see you as a highly successful twenty-six-year-old guy. You have to let them know you have problems and that you're human. You look like you think you're better than them.' He was right. As soon as I started talking about my problems, they left me alone.

And he helped me get strong enough to divorce my first wife without a lot of baggage. I gave her whatever we had in the bank, $25,000 in stocks, and some cash. I didn't have to pay alimony, and she got married in six months; she had two or three husbands after me.

FAREWELL, CINDERELLA

Starting in about 2006, Ilene began to notice a little bit of a memory problem when she started to make even some simple recipes. She's forget the ingredients, and I'd have to remind her. It was rather subtle in the beginning of the memory problem. This continued on through the year in a very mild way, and we'd both kid, "Oh, we're both getting older," and leave it at that.

But in 2007 she had an incident in her car. She drove up on the top of one of the Valley roads that leads to the ocean, which is very high up. She pulled into a little parking place there, and she said it was like she woke up and didn't remember how she drove there. Obviously, this was very disturbing to both of us. It hadn't happened before, so we put it down to the fact that she had started to take Ambien at night. She had become restless, going to sleep, and we thought maybe it was the result of the drug.

So she stopped taking that, and there weren't any more incidents like that. There were still problems with remembering recipes and phone numbers, but there was no reason for me to think there was anything more than advancing age, like we all have, to some degree. I went to Skidmore Institute that summer, where I was the artistic director. It was my twentieth year, and they gave me a very nice plaque and all of that. When I came back, Ilene had done okay by herself, but she said, for the very first time in our entire marriage, "Do you think, honey, next time you could go for just one week instead of two?"

And I said, "Oh, sure, I'll be glad to do that." It so happened from that summertime, when I returned, things got a little more serious, and I did not go back to Skidmore again. Ilene had not driven much while I was away, maybe to the grocery store once or twice, but when I got in the car with her, it was really maddening, because she was hesitant with turning and making decisions. This was a girl who had a sporting attitude about driving. She had driven race cars when she was younger, back in Long Island, and she was a very sure and confident driver. She could even drive a shift car—the best of anyone I've ridden with. But she was having trouble now.

So I said, "Honey, I don't think you should drive anymore," and fortunately, she said, "I don't think so either." It was really tough. She had this beautiful bright-red Mustang with a tan canvas top, and she just loved that car—she really did—and she had been a wonderful driver, prior to these problems.

After the driving incident, I realized something serious was going on, and I took her to a neurologist. I thought he was a good doctor, but he asked her a few questions, such as her age and address, which she answered correctly, and that seemed to be enough for him to say, "Oh, well, you don't have Alzheimer's or anything like that." We walked out of the office, and I felt pretty good. I found out later how wrong he was. She really had the very definite onset of the early stages of Alzheimer's. Something like her driving was a very good clue, I found out later.

I did a lot of reading and researching on the web, so I was pretty convinced she was in the early stages. By then, cooking was getting to be extra tough, and I was helping out in the kitchen. A few times I would say, "Let me make a simple dinner or a frozen dinner," and she was glad of that. She was such a good homemaker that it was embarrassing for her to ask, "What goes next?"

I tried to treat it lightly. It got to the point, though, where I did all the cooking, and I, of course, am not a cook. I'm a drummer. If you tasted what I cook, you'd know I'm a drummer. She was very good; she was so patient. I would buy good dinners by Stouffer's and Marie Callender's, and I was the king of the microwave. Maybe once in a while I'd put something into the oven, but we didn't cook anything from scratch anymore. I made my mind up by October 2007 to call Skidmore College to tell them that I would not be coming the next summer. I felt it was final that I stay with her on a regular basis. I canceled one or two other jobs I had for later in the year, where I had to get on a plane, because I felt it was time for steady caregiving. I was right, of course.

It was so funny that that first diagnosis from a supposedly good neurologist steered us off a while, but it became quite apparent that she was getting a little deeper into the Alzheimer's. And when I took her in for a physical checkup, even our family doctor said to me quietly, when I asked him about it, that he thought she definitely had it, even though he was not a neurology specialist. By this time she was having trouble with our address and phone number.

When you love someone so much, it doesn't mean anything to cancel work. I had work for 2008 and even some for 2009, but it didn't matter. It just seemed important to take care of her. I think that's the natural feeling you have when you love somebody a lot. I felt a little bad about Skidmore, because Skidmore was one of the nicest experiences I had ever had for twenty years. I love teaching kids, and we would teach the cream-of-the-crop high school kids from the Northeast. They had to audition with tapes and things, and we had a wonderful time for two weeks each summer, but I did do twenty years of it.

We moved along through 2008, and we could go to a movie once in a while. Her attention span was getting a little less when we'd be in the movie, but she wouldn't stop me from watching it. And we'd go out to dinner at her favorite places, like Red Lobster and Chili's. She also liked those iced mocha drinks they make at Gelson's Market, which is two minutes from our house, and we'd sit there and people watch for an hour, enjoying the weather. The other favorite thing to do was for me to drive her around to look at the flower arrangements at people's homes, because she had been a real gardener before the illness took over. We would take nature rides. I tried to take her to the beach one time, but when we got on the canyon road, which is very narrow, she panicked, so I had to turn around.

The disease was pretty slow and gradual, although she would sleep a lot. She would need help getting dressed and after breakfast, she would go over to the couch and before you'd know it, she was asleep. Because a lot of older Alzheimer's people fall a lot, I was always terrified to leave her for any length of time. I hired a professional nurse to come when I had to go grocery shopping and things. The nurse said to me, "You can't watch them all the time, but we try. I've had it where I've left the room for thirty seconds, and the woman fell and hit her head. I felt awful, but I had to go to the bathroom."

I'd sit in the kitchen and read or have the television on softly. She'd sleep, or we'd have dinner. I'd like to mention to anyone going through this, there are two drugs that are highly touted to slow down Alzheimer's: Aricept and Namenda. We tried both of those drugs, one at a time, and they spun her around, mentally. She begged me never to give her either of them again. She said, "Honey, I feel as though I'm going crazy. The earth is swimming, and I'm panicking." They have very good results with other people, though. A doctor I spoke with later said that one out of every ten people cannot take either one of those drugs.

I want to mention Leeza's Place, a gathering place started by Leeza

107

Gibbons. Her mom got Alzheimer's some years ago and had it for ten years. Leeza found, as many of us do, that when a loved one has this disease, we don't know much of what to do. I had read in a magazine about Leeza's Place, where caregivers could go and even bring their loved ones with them. The staff would look after the loved ones, play games with them, or sing songs, and the caregivers would have a meeting in a closed room. I went down to Leeza's Place and met a wonderful girl named Stephanie Elkins, who said, "I think it would be good for you. I can tell you're very upset about this, and you need companionship with other people like you. Don't be a caregiver and isolate yourself."

She's a very smart girl. I really liked the vibe there, and I took Ilene down there around the middle of 2008. Judy, an older lady, played Frank Sinatra records, and my wife loved that. They would dance together, and she was great at keeping Ilene happy for about an hour and a half while we had a caregivers meeting.

I want to recommend this for anyone who has an Alzheimer's loved one. You need help; you need to talk to other people who are putting their energy and time into looking after someone, because you learn so much from them. I met a wonderful man named Sandy. He had been at it already a few years, and I learned a lot.

You don't learn just about the patient and how to do more for the patient, but you learn about yourself. Leeza Gibbons wrote a book called *Take the Oxygen First*. The whole idea of that is to not let yourself get too depressed or too run down, physically and mentally, from the 24/7 care that you're probably giving to your loved one. I took a lot of this to heart, although it took me quite a while. I don't think I took a day for myself for six months. I just stayed in and watched Ilene, and took Ilene out, but I finally hired the nurse one day when I didn't have to go grocery shopping—I just went out and drove around. I got a little fast-food lunch and sat in the park for a while, just for a change. That's what they mean: you've got to do something for yourself. I recommend Leeza Gibbons's book highly. She loved her mother dearly. Her mother was a very loving and strong personality, but she descended into Alzheimer's, and she had it for ten years. For anyone reading this book, go on the web and check out Leeza's Place. They helped me so much with the feeling of being alone. It's so important to talk to people who are going through the same thing.

On January 29, 2009, I turned eighty years old, and the five drummers I'd been having lunches with gave me a nice birthday celebration lunch. My friend Bill Selditz organized it, and he had the most beautiful chocolate cake made. Although our get-togethers were usually guys only, once a month or so, I asked them if I could bring Ilene because of her condition. They were so great and said, "Oh, sure." She got all dressed up in a sharp black dress, with her white pearls, and she looked so beautiful. Most of them didn't realize she had Alzheimer's, because she didn't talk too much, and she was a charming woman, although I had told them. She answered simple questions when they asked her, and a lot of them were kidding me about getting older and this and that. She didn't have a lot to do, but she enjoyed being there so very much. The guys were great, and Jeff Hamilton gave me a wonderful album of some records I had made with Oliver Nelson, and Paul Kreibich did, too, as did Joe La Barbera. It was a wonderful birthday. The luncheon day actually fell on my birthday, and it was so very nice, especially because I had my wife with me. It was the last type of thing like that we went to.

Throughout that year, it was very hard to get her to go to bed at night—I think that was because there had been one or two instances of bedwetting. I think she was so traumatized by that, she didn't want to go to bed. I would cajole, "Oh honey, please. Everything will be fine," but it became such a job to get her to go to sleep. Outside of the difficulty to get her to sleep, there weren't problems, and we were getting along fine with my microwave cooking and going out occasionally. We got through 2009.

Starting into 2010 was the beginning of the end for my dear wife. I'll never forget the day—it's burned into my brain—February 15, when she got dressed nice, and I told her I would take her out to dinner to her favorite place, the Red Lobster. She liked the waitress over there named Daisy, who we had been friendly with for a number of years. I started our usual routine of pulling the car out of the garage. As usual, I came and got her, took her out to the car, and she stood by the side of the car on the passenger side. Next I would open the door and help her in, but this time, as I turned to open the door, I heard this terrible sound, almost like the crack of a bat on a baseball. She had fallen, just like a tree falls in a forest, and hit her head on the concrete driveway. She broke her glasses—she was wearing great big sunglasses, which may have actually helped her a little, because otherwise, she might have hit her eye on the edge of the concrete. Her eyes were rolled back, and she was semiconscious. I became so completely terrified, that I pulled out my cell phone and couldn't even press the right buttons. So I ran in the house and took one of the portable phones and called 911. In less than ten minutes, the fire truck from Calabasas came, and the paramedics were great. She had come back to consciousness, and her face was already showing the bruising, but they were so great. They put a little neck brace on her, and they put her on a stretcher and said, "Mr. Shaughnessy, why don't you follow us to West Hills Hospital?" And that's what we did. I was terrified because I knew she had hit her head—as if she needed that with everything else she had going on. But I was glad she didn't put her eye out because of the way she fell, with the side of her glasses at the edge of the driveway, going to the grass. We went to emergency and by then, she was conscious. She had a brain scan, and the emergency people were just great to her. The word came down that nothing major had happened, and she could be discharged. Within about three hours, they were wheeling her out to my car to go home.

I couldn't believe it, actually. It seemed too good to be true that she could be released so quickly. As it turned out, it was too good to be true. We got home, and she was able, with my help, to get out of my car and slowly walk into the house. She was too knocked out to go upstairs to sleep and asked if she could sleep on the couch, which of course was fine. I covered her up and put a pillow under her head. I slept in the same room on the recliner chair. But by the next morning, she couldn't walk. And her face looked atrocious—black, blue, and yellow—yet she said she didn't feel bad. Because she couldn't walk or go to the bathroom, I ordered a hospital bed right away, and they brought it over that same day.

During this period, I worked one jazz festival down near San Diego, subbing for my late friend Jake Hanna, who had wanted me to sub for him before he died. When he passed away, I wanted to do a good job for Jake. He was a good friend of mine, and I admired him a great deal as a drummer and as a person. I had that festival to go to and I felt terrible, but I called the nurse that had watched Ilene before, and she said, "Ed, I'm going to be here twenty-four hours a day. There's nothing more you can do for her than I can't do. I'm a trained nurse. She's not suffering anything bad, other than she can't walk. I've taken care of her before, and I will take care of her now."

I did the festival and despite how well the nurse looked after Ilene for the three days, she still developed some bed sores, so I felt she should go to the hospital. Around March 1, I made arrangements for her to go back. They did another brain scan, but they couldn't find anything. She stayed there for three days, and at the end of that time, I knew she had to go to a nursing facility. I would have been happy to look after her, but I wouldn't have been capable of keeping her free from the bed sores. She needed professional care, so after my son and I scouted three places, I arranged for her to go to Canyon Oaks Nursing. They looked after her with a lot of heart and care, and I would go see her every day and bring her an iced mocha. Gradually, however, bit by bit, from March 1, through April, May, and June, her recognition faculties went away. I don't think she knew who I was or who Danny was. He came twice a week from work and on the weekend. I would still visit and talk to her, but by April or May, she didn't know me. She didn't seem to be suffering, but eventually, by the end of June, she stopped eating and drinking. She had always told me, long before she ever had gotten ill, "Don't ever have them put tubes in me and keep me alive with tubes. We tried that with my mother, and it was horrible because she died anyway."

So I acquiesced to her wishes. I called hospice at the advice of our wonderful doctor, and they were just great. Her eyes would still somehow light up when she'd see us. And the last thing she said to me was two weeks before she passed away, when I said to her, "It's so good to see you, honey," and she looked at me, just like the old days, and said, "Oh, it's so good to see you too, honey." And I almost fell down because she hadn't been talking much. It was great.

On July 1, I was getting ready to go see her about noon, as I did daily and was glad to do, and the phone rang. The hospice lady said, "Mr. Shaughnessy, I think your wife is near the end." I said, "I'll hurry right over," and she said, "No, don't hurry; just wait a minute." She left the phone, came back, and said, "Mr. Shaughnessy, your wife has gone to sleep for good; she passed away. That's why I didn't want you to rush over here. I knew she was near the end. She just went to sleep."

I finished dressing and went over, and she was sleeping peacefully. I sat for about half an hour, holding her hand, and then I kissed her and left. I had already made arrangements for her cremation, which is what she had wanted. She didn't want any kind of a funeral service, because she didn't like those things. I'm still waiting to get the nerve up, though, to go with my son to scatter her ashes on the same cliffs where we scattered our son Jimmy's ashes, which is where Ilene asked to be.

I had the most wonderful life for forty-seven years. She was the light of my life. My life went onto a new plane when I married her. She was the most wonderful person. She was generous, gentle, brave when she had to be, and such a loving mother to her two sons. And she put up with me and some of my problems for some years, and then I got straightened out, I'm glad to say. She left a legacy of love and caring. And there are so many people who loved her for being the voice of Cinderella. I still hear from people who tell me how much her singing and speaking voice meant to them when they were kids, and so many young girls will still enjoy it. That's what Ilene used to say: "I think it's wonderful that after I'm gone, children will still be able to enjoy my voice, singing and speaking as Cinderella."

So we'll say good-bye to Cinderella for now in this book. I was so proud to have you for my wife.

DANNY

I want to say a few words about Danny, because he's such a wonderful son, and he's been such a comfort since my dear wife, his mother, passed away last year. He was so helpful during that time. He insisted that I didn't go seven times a week to see Ilene. He made sure to go whenever he could, whenever he was off from work. Sometimes he would take half a day off from work. He said, "Dad, I don't want you to get burned out. You've got to take a day off. I don't care if you sit around and watch basketball." He was so understanding. And it was good to have a break. I learned it's important when you're caregiving that you take a little time for yourself—not a lot but a little. My son was so good about that, and he helped me so much with that. He was a tower of strength during those times.

Dan is such a great person, and I'm very proud of him. I've heard this from many people who have worked under him at about four different hotels in the Marriott group. As he moved up the corporate ladder, he sometimes would change hotels for a new position. I'm very proud, too, that he is very much a self-made man. He had about six months of business school at Cal State

Northridge and then came to us and said, "I have a chance to work at the little Holiday Inn on Ventura Boulevard, and to tell you the truth, I think it may be a better thing for me to learn the hotel business that way than to stay in business school."

I thought he made a lot of sense, because I am sort of a self-made drummer, aside from friends and a teacher or two, but mostly a lot of it on my own. I thought it was okay. I said, "You know, you can always go back to school if you want to," and he said, "That's the way I feel. School will be there."

He started working at the Holiday Inn in Woodland Hills. They put him behind the counter because he had an affable, personable style, and he's a big, tall (six foot three), good-looking guy—really handsome, if I say so myself. I think he was only there a couple of months when the boss who ran the place said, "You're so good with people. I'm going to make you my sales manager, and you're going to go around and get us some business."

Dan thought that sounded great, and I heard later, when a lady from the Hilton came to steal him away, that she got sick and tired of losing accounts to that big, tall, handsome guy from the Holiday Inn, who always had chocolate chip cookies for the secretaries. I thought that was a great story. He found out that leaving a gift of some chocolate chip cookies always got you remembered by the secretaries, who often would make the reservations for people coming in from out of town, He got a lot of business that way. Finally the lady who got tired of his stealing her accounts hired him, and it was definitely a more prestigious job at the Hilton. But he was always grateful to the Holiday Inn because he learned a lot there.

He worked at the Hilton for a couple of years, and then some Marriott people heard about him, and a big Marriott stole him away with a better position. That became his very long association, which I think is now close to twenty years. He is now in charge of marketing and sales at the beautiful Renaissance Hotel in Hollywood. I've been there and played there on my eighty-second birthday. He started a jazz brunch a couple of years ago, and I had never played it because I didn't want nepotism to raise its head. But we had a great celebration there for my eighty-second birthday, with my quintet, and he had a great big cake made that was about four feet by two feet, with a picture of me behind the drums on it.

Dan has been a very good athlete over his life, and he loves music. He can sing great, too. He actually sang "The Star-Spangled Banner" at a Clippers game and knocked everybody out. Thank goodness his mother was able to attend that. It was only a couple of years ago before she took ill. I was away working.

He has a wonderful wife named Nicah and a stepdaughter named Amarah, who just turned eighteen. I can't say enough wonderful things about his wife. She has such a big heart. When my dear wife got sick, Nicah would go visit her and do her nails and her hair and things that made my wife happy. She called it a "beauty visit," and it made my wife smile. I was so grateful because I couldn't do those things for her, even though I would go to see her every day. And she made special tapes of Ilene's favorite music and brought them in to play by her bed. She did so many thoughtful things for her. I love her dearly. I couldn't have a daughter of my own that I love any more than I do Nicah.

I am so grateful to have them. It's the only family I have, and I want to take good care of myself to be around for a lot of years, because I'm the only family now that Dan has too. He's a wonderful, wonderful guy.

KEEPING YOUR CHOPS UP
IN LATER YEARS

I'd like to talk about how tough it is, as you get older and you still like to play, but you don't play anywhere as often as you used to play. In my case, one of the reasons I don't play as often as I used to play is that many of the people who used to hire me are now retired or have passed on. Particularly in the school area, I'm so thrilled that I get a call once in a while. Recently I went to the University of Wisconsin to do three shows with their fantastic director Mike Leckrone, who puts 250-piece marching band on stage in chairs. We play Duke Ellington and Count Basie—I'm so grateful to get calls like that.

I've found out through trial and error—plenty of error—that I have to practice regularly. I practice every day at home, because I have to try to fill in that gap of not working regularly. For instance, when I did the Tonight Show, I did that five days a week, and very often I would be working something else with Doc on the weekend or something of my own. It wouldn't be unusual for me to be playing seven days a week. Frankly, when you're playing seven days a week, you really don't have to do a lot of practicing. When you play so often, you keep a certain level of dexterity, technique, endurance, and everything else.

I've found out that I haven't slowed down a bit as far as technique, speed, and dexterity, but that the endurance factor is what I lose the most. I didn't play much at all during the near three-year period I was looking after Ilene. I turned down most of the work that was offered to me, and I was glad to do that. But when I started to get back into drumming, I realized the endurance factor was a big factor. I realized I had to practice harder at home. I have a practice set at home that doesn't make a lot of noise, and I practice hard on that. Then I sit down at a slightly muffled set of drums, a sort of two-way practice—playing on rubber pads and quiet pedals for hard practice and endurance and a muscular thing, and then going to a regular drum set that is muffled, because I don't have a real practice room. I haven't ever had any complaints. I never want to bother people. I found out you can muffle the drums up a little bit and still get a lot of work done, and it doesn't bother anybody. I've been in this house close to thirty years without a complaint.

A guy playing a brass instrument, for instance, who doesn't stay at that horn every day and only works occasionally, like I'm doing now, would have it really tough. You have to practice to keep it up. You have to balance out, with more continuous practice, what you had normally been doing from more continuous work—it's as simple as that.

At one job I had at a festival not too long ago, playing with a very big, powerful band with eleven brass and six or seven saxophones—an adult band—I found out that I was hard-pressed to drive that band the way I usually drove a band like Doc's all the time, because I really hadn't played quite that hard in a while. I got through it okay; everybody liked it, but I didn't like it. I realized after that, that I was going to practice harder, more for endurance. You've got to have that, particularly for big band, not as much for small band. You play much lighter for small band, and if your dexterity is good, you get by fine. When you're the heart of a big band, and it's driving music, the drummer has to dig in to make it happen, and then you have to have that endurance.

Like they say, old dogs, new tricks. I'm learning because it's something different. I've never had this before in my life. I always played so much. I always practiced a lot. I always practiced on the Tonight Show, too. When everybody went to have coffee or get something to eat, I sat up there and practiced. But the point is, you don't need it in the same way you do when you're not working regularly. The drums and the music deserve all the time and the practice, because they've been awfully good to me, but if I want it to stay good to me, I have to do my part. So I'm doing that and happy to do it.

I would like to sum up how very grateful I am to jazz and music for having such a wonderful life. I have had the chance to play some symphonic music with orchestras as well as playing with some of the amazing jazz greats and then, of course, with the superb Doc Severinsen's big band for twenty-nine years. It was such a great opportunity with that band. I had so many wonderful experiences that I am just grateful, grateful, grateful. I think whatever hard work and study I put in, which was considerable, was very small compared to the rewards I reaped. I would like to encourage anyone reading this book to stick to your guns, be persistent, and you will achieve your goals. Of course, you always have to have a modicum of talent, but a great deal of hard work and perseverance go into it, too.

In the very turbulent times we are in right now, in the 2000-years, I still think it's the same as it has been in our country for such a long time. You can come from humble circumstances, as did I and many others did, and you can be successful, and it doesn't depend on where you came from or how much you had. More important is your ambition, what you're seeking to achieve, and your ability to do hard work. I hope it doesn't sound naive, but I really believe we are so lucky to live in a country where you can do that, where you can come from humble circumstances. I remember people telling me in Jersey when I was young and just starting out, "Nobody'll ever let you in, not in New York. It's a closed shop." So much negativity. Clearly, they were people who had never tried it. I, on the contrary, found a very welcoming and helpful attitude from many of the great New York musicians, of all colors, all persuasions. When my sincerity about the music was known, that was the "open sesame" of their good treatment. It was the mutual love of the music that united us and brought us together.

I am so grateful to music and to drums. I remember my friend Tony Williams, who we lost way too early, once said during a concert, "You know I really love these drums. These drums have taken me all over the world and have let me play with some of the greatest people." And he went over and patted his drums. He was so sincere, and I feel just that same way. I just love these drums, and I've always felt I have a debt to my instrument to practice and play well all the time—not just to people, not just for my career or my ego.

Look how good the instrument has been to you, so you should be good to it, and practice a lot, and get to play well, and take pride in it. That's what I've tried to do for many years. I'm still trying to do it; it's just a little harder when you're a geezer. I'm still trying, and I'll still keep plugging.

I want to wish the very best to any musician who is trying to achieve his or her goals. Any time you see me and would like to talk, the door is always open. I've always been that way, and I will always be that way. I really love to talk with—and help, if I can—any younger musicians who come my way. I never forget that everybody did it for me. I'm just repaying a very deserving debt in trying to help others, and that's one of the beautiful things about our world of music. You'll find a great deal of it, as did I.   The great worlds of jazz and big band gave "the kid with the wagon" a wonderful ride through life.

INDEX

Appendix 1: Discography

The total number of albums that Ed Shaughnessy appears on is well over 500, but it would be very difficult at this point to compile a comprehensive list. The albums listed here represent an overview of Ed's recording career.

Trigger Alpert	*Trigger Happy!* (1956)	Drums
Gene Ammons	*Gene Ammons' Story: Gentle Jug* (1961)	
Gene Ammons	*Soulful Moods of Gene Ammons* (1962)	Drums
Gene Ammons	*Gentle Jug*	Drums
Various Artists	*Atlantic Jazz Vocals: Voices of...* (1994)	Drums
Various Artists	*Atlantic Jazz: Singers* (1947)	Drums
Count Basie	*Broadway Basie's Way* (1967)	Drums
Various Artists	*Beat Generation* (1992)	Drums
Tony Bennett	*Jazz* (1954)	Drums
George Benson	*Verve Jazz Masters 21* (1968)	Drums
George Benson	*Other Side of Abbey Road* (1969)	Drums
Irving Berlin	*Irving Berlin Always*	Drums
Various Artists	*Big Band Hit Parade* (1988) Cincinnati Symphony	Drums
Stephen Bishop	*Bish* (1978)	Drums
Patti Bown	*Plays Big Piano* (1960)	
Bob Brookmeyer	*Dual Role of Bob Brookmeyer* (1954)	Drums
Bob Brookmeyer	*Revelation* (1964)	Drums
Various Artists	*Burning for Buddy: A Tribute to Buddy Rich* (1994)	Drums
Gary Burton	*Groovy Sound of Music* (1964)	Drums
Lodi Carr	*Lady Bird* (1992)	Drums
Betty Carter	*'Round Midnight* [Atlantic] (1962)	Drums
Teddy Charles with Shorty...	*Collaboration: West* (1952)	Drums
Teddy Charles with Jimmy...	*New Directions, Vol. 1* (1952)	Drums
Teddy Charles	*New Directions, Vol. 2* [With Hall Overton] (1953)	Drums
Teddy Charles Tentet	*Tentet* (1956)	
Teddy Charles	*Word from Bird* (1957)	Drums
Teddy Charles	*On Campus!* (1959)	Drums
Cincinnati Pops Orchestra	*Crossover/Puttin' on the Ritz* (1995)	Drums
Various Artists	*Complete Johnny Mercer Songbook* (1998)	Drums
Chris Connor	*Sings the George Gershwin Almanac...* (1956)	Drums
Chris Connor	*Jazz Date with Chris Connor/Chris...* (1956)	Drums
Chris Connor	*Chris Craft* (1958)	Drums
Chris Connor	*Chris Connor at the Village Gate* (1963)	Drums
DJ Uncle Al	*Liberty City* (1996)	Drums
Various Artists	*Debut Records Story* (1952)	Drums
Roy Eldridge	*Roy Eldridge in Paris*	Drums
Les & Larry Elgart	*Sophisticated Swing: Best of the...* (1992)	Drums
Various Artists	*Erteguns' New York Cabaret* (1987)	Drums
The Flow	*Flow* (1970)	Percussion
Jimmy Forrest	*Soul Street* (1961)	Drums
Various Artists	*Gentle Duke: The Ellington Soloists Play Duke* (1997)	Drums
Jimmy Giuffre	*Complete Capitol & Atlantic...* (1954)	Drums
Jimmy Giuffre	*Jimmy Giuffre/Music Man* (1999)	Drums
Benny Goodman	*King of Swing 1958-1967* (1995)	Drums
Honi Gordon	*Honi Gordon Sings* (1962)	Drums
David Grisman	*Dawg Grass / Dawg Jazz* (1982)	Drums

Arlo Guthrie	*Arlo* (1968)	Drums, Tabla
Arlo Guthrie	*Last of the Brooklyn Cowboys*	Drums, Tabla
Various Artists	*Hit Jazz* (1997)	Drums
Billie Holliday	*Lady in Autumn: The Best of the...*(1946)	Drums
Billie Holliday	*Billie Holliday Songbook* (1952)	Drums
Billie Holliday	*Stay with Me* (1959)	Drums
Billie Holliday	*History of the Real Billie Holliday* (1986)	
Billie Holliday	*Billie's Best* (1992)	Drums
Billie Holliday	*Verve Jazz Masters 12: Billie Holiday* (1994)	Drums
Billie Holliday	*First issue: The Great American Songbook* (1994)	Drums
Billie Holliday	*Billie Holliday Story, Vol. 3*	Drums
Various Artists	*Impulsively Ellington!: A Tribute To Duke Ellington* (1999)	Drums, Vibraphone
Jackie and Roy	*Jackie & Roy* (1993)	Drums
Various Artists	*Jazz Big Names, Vol. 2* (1996)	Drums
Various Artists	*Jazz 'round Midnight: Trumpet* (1992)	Drums
Various Artists	*Jazz Vocal Essentials, Vol. 1* (1999)	Drums
Various Artists	*Jazz for Lovers* [Prestige] (1957)	Drums
Various Artists	*Jingle Bell Jazz* (1959)	Drums
Etta Jones	*From the Heart* (1962)	Drums
Etta Jones	*Lonely and Blue* (1962)	Drums
Quincy Jones	*Jazz 'Round Midnight* (1958)	Drums
Quincy Jones	*Plays Hip Hits* (1963)	Drums
Quincy Jones	*Pawnbroker/The Deadly Affair*	Percussion
Quincy Jones & His Orchestra		
	Pure Delight: The Essence of Quincy Jones & His Orchestra 1953–1964(1995)	
Rahsaan Roland Kirk	*Complete Recordings of Roland Kirk* (1961)	Drums
Lee Konitz	*Ezz-Thetic* (1951)	Drums
Erich Kunzel & The...	*Very Best of Erich Kunzel: Top 20* (1994)	Drums
Arnie Lawrence	*Inside an Hour Glass*	
Hubert Laws	*Crying Song* (1970)	Tabla
Jack Lemmon	*Piano and Vocals* (1990)	Drums
Mundell Lowe Quartet	*Mundell Lowe Quartet* (1955)	Drums
Mundell Lowe	*Guitar Moods*	Drums
Mundell Lowe	*New Music of Alec Wilder*	Drums
Various Artists	*Lusty Moods* (1965)	Drums
Various Artists	*Masters of Jazz, Vol. 6: Male Vocal Classics*	Drums
Various Artists	*Masters of Jazz, Vol. 5: Female Vocal Classics* (1937)	Drums
Various Artists	*Masters of Jazz, Vol. 7: Johnny Griffin*	Drums
Johnny Mathis	*Johnny Mathis* (1957)	Drums
Johnny Mathis	*Johnny Mathis 40th Anniversary Edition* (1996)	Drums
Carmen McRae	*Ultimate Carmen McRae* (1964)	Drums
Lucky Millinder	*Big Band Hits* (1956)	
Charles Mingus	*Passions of a Man: The Complete Mingus...*	Drums
Wes Montgomery	*Road Song* (1968)	Drums
Maria Muldaur	*Maria Muldau*r (1974)	Drums
Oliver Nelson	*Afro-American Sketches*	Drums
Oliver Nelson	*Verve Jazz Masters, Vol. 48*	Drums
Tommy Newsom	*Tommy Newsom and His TV Jazz Stars* (1990)	Drums
Tommy Newsom & L.A.	*I Remember You, Johnny* (1996)	Drums
Charlie Parker	*Complete Stage/ Live Performances* (1994)	Drums
Perez Prado	*Mambo Mania/Havana 3 A.M.* (1990)	Drums
Perez Prado	*Voodoo Suite/Exotic Suite* (1990)	Drums
Arthur Prysock	*Jazz 'round Midnight* (1995)	Drums

Arthur Prysock	*Compact Jazz*	Drums
Original Soundtrack	*Quiz Show* (1994)	Drums
Johnnie Ray	*Cry* [Bear Family Box Set] (1990)	Drums
Johnnie Ray	*High Drama: The Real Johnnie Ray*	Drums
Various Artists	*Realhot Jazz* (1982)	Drums
Marty Robbins	*Essential Marty Robbins: 1951-1982* (1991)	Drums
Marty Robbins	*Country 1951-1958* (1991)	Drums
Various Artists	*Sampler of Dixie/Bop Jazz 1927-1949*	Drums
Shirley Scott	*Roll 'em*	Drums
Various Artists	*Sentimental Journey: Pop Vocal...* (1995)	Drums
Doc Severinsen	*Great Arrival*	Drums
Doc Severinsen & The...	*Tonight Show Band: World Premier...*	Drums
The Tonight Show Band	*Tonight Show Band, Vol. 2*	Drums
Doc Severinsen	*Good Medicine* (1992)	Drums
Doc Serverinsen & The...	*Merry Christmas from Doc* (1992)	Drums
Doc Severinsen	*Swingin' the Blues*	Drums
Ravi Shankar	*In Celebration*	Drums
Bobby Short	*50 by Bobby Short*	Drums
Zoot Sims	*First Recordings!* (1950)	Drums
Zoot Sims/Tony Scott/Al...	*East Coast Sounds*	Drums
Jimmy Smith	*Bashin': The Unpredictable Jimmy...* (1962)	Drums
Jimmy Smith	*Any Number Can Win* (1963)	Drums
Sam "The Man" Taylor	*Bad and the Beautiful* (1962)	Drums
Clark Terry	*Color Changes* (1960)	Drums
Clark Terry	*Mellow Moods* (1961)	Drums
Clark Terry	*Plays the Jazz Version of "All...* (1962)	Drums
Cal Tjader	*Talkin' Verve: Roots of Acid Jazz* (1961)	Drums
Cal Tjader	*Several Shades of Jade/Breeze from* (1963)	Drums
Cal Tjader	*Warm Wave* (1964)	Drums
Cal Tjader	*Verve Jazz Masters, Vol. 39*	Drums
Tonight Show Band w/ Doc Severinsen	*"Once More with Feeling"*	Drums
Tonight Show Band w/ Doc Severinsen	*"Swingin' the Blues"*	Drums
Various Artists	*Unos Dos Tres: Latin Jazz Grooves*	Drums
Charlie Ventura Septet	*Charlie Ventura In Concert...*	Drums
Chuck Wayne/Brew Moore	*Tasty Pudding* (1953)	Drums
Chuck Wayne featuring Zoot Sims & Brew Moore	*Jazz Guitarist* (1953)	Drums

ED'S FAVORITES

"the CD's that I like best as examples of my work."

'DOC' SEVERINSEN BAND
   1. *SWINGIN' THE BLUES*
   2. *ONCE MORE WITH FEELINGS*

COUNT BASIE BAND
   1. *BROADWAY, BASIE'S WAY*
   2. *SHOW TIME*
   3. *HOLLYWOOD, BASIE'S WAY*

OLIVER NELSON
   1. *AFRO-AMERICAN SKETCHES*
   2. *JAZZHATTAN SUITE*

JIMMY SMITH BIG BAND
   BASHING

ED SHAUGHNESSY QUINTET
   JAZZ IN THE POCKET

CLARK TERRY
   COLOR CHANGES

TEDDY CHARLES
   WORD FROM BIRD

CINCINNATI POPS
   BIG BAND HIT PARADE

CHARLIE VENTURA
   IN CONCERT – PASADENA 1949

Late 1940s

Slingerland		Zildjian	
A	5x14	1	14 hihats
B,C	9x13	2	20 crash-ride
D	7x6 Bongo	3	22 ride
E	12x20		
F	14x20		
G	16x16		
H	16x14		

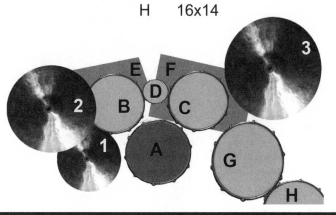

Early 1950s

Slingerland, Zildjian

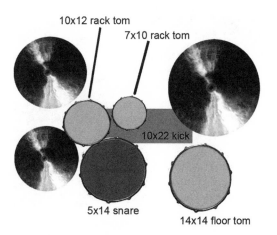

10x12 rack tom

7x10 rack tom

10x22 kick

5x14 snare

14x14 floor tom

Late 1950s

Slingerland		Zildjian	
A	5x14	1	14 hihats
B	9x13	2	18 crash
C	7x10	3	22 ride
D	14x14	4	18 ride
E	12x16		
F	14x20		

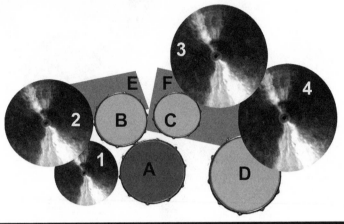

1960s (Ed endorsed Slingerland until 1962)

Slingerland		Zildjian	
A	5x14	1	14 Hihats
B	9x13	2	18 Crash
C	16x14	3	22 Ride
D	16x16		
E	14x24		

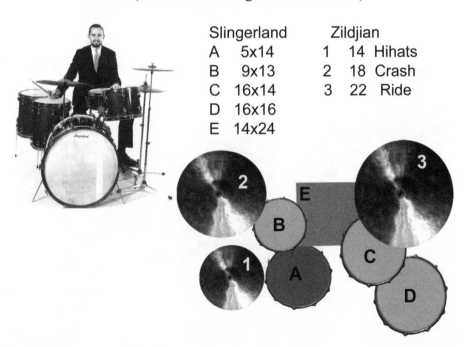

1972-1976
Pearl

A   5x14
B   8x12
C   9x13
D   9x13
E   10x14
F   16x16
G   16x18
H   14x20
I   14x22
Zildjian
1   14 Hihats
2   18 Crash
3   20 Crash
4   22 Ride
5   18 Crash

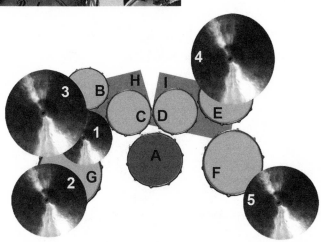

1977-2004 Ludwig

A	5x14 Black Beauty	I	16x18
B	16x18	J	14x22
C	6x6	K	14x24
D	6x8	1	14 hihats
E	8x10	2	18 Crash
F	9x13	3	18 Crash
G	8x12	4	21 Ride
H	16x16	5	16 Crash

Zildjian cymbals
until about 1981,
then switched to
Sabian

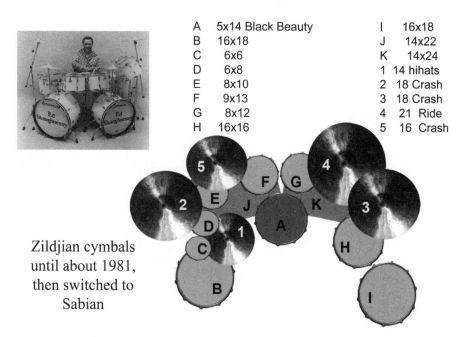

Since 2004 most of Ed's kits have closely resembled the gear profiled by Modern Drummer magazine in 2004, diagrammed below.

Ludwig drums, Sabian cymbals.

Heads: Snare batter 14" medium white Aquarian, Classic clear on tom batters, Ludwig heavy clears on bottoms. Aquarian super-kick 2 on bass drum batters with Ludwig coated on fronts.

Ludwig hardware with legless hi-hat, chain drive pedals with Danmar beaters.

Pro-Mark sticks; Shaughnessy 707 model.

RhythmTech Mambo and Cha cha bells.

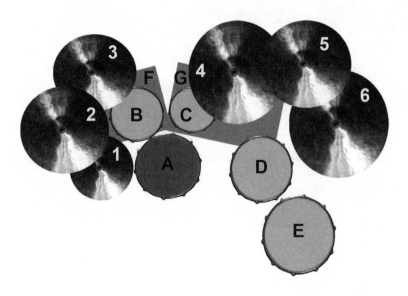

Ludwig
A   5x14 Black Beauty
B   9x13
C   7x12
D   14x16
E   16x16
F   14x22
G   14x24

Sabian
1   15" AA hihats
2   18" AA Med-Th Crash
3   15" AA Med-Th Crash
4   21" Signature Ride Med-Hvy
5   18" AA Med-Th Crash
6   22" AA Chinese

REBEATS PUBLICATIONS

THE ROGERS BOOK
by Rob Cook
Business history,
dating guide

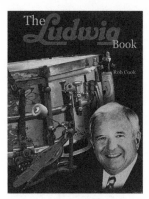

THE LUDWIG BOOK
by Rob Cook
Business history,
dating guide

**THE MAKING OF A
DRUM COMPANY**
The autobiography of
Wm. F. Ludwig II,
with Rob Cook

**THE SLINGERLAND
BOOK**
by Rob Cook
Business history,
dating guide

**HAL BLAINE & THE
WRECKING CREW**
Autobiography of Hal Blaine,
with Mr. Bonzai

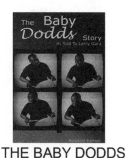

**THE BABY DODDS
STORY**
Autobiography of Baby Dodds,
as told to Larry Gara

**GENE KRUPA, HIS
LIFE AND TIMES**
biography of Gene Krupa,
by Bruce Crowther

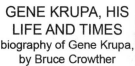

**TRAPS, THE DRUM
WONDER**
biography of Buddy Rich,
by Mel Torme

REBEATS PUBLICATIONS

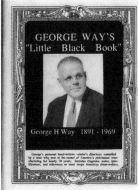

GEORGE WAY'S LITTLE BLACK BOOK
capsule biography & reproduction of Way's personal notebook

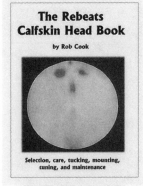

THE REBEATS CALFSKIN HEAD BOOK
by Rob Cook

GRETSCH SERIAL NUMBER DATING GUIDE
by Rick Gier

DRUM COLORS: THE REBEATS COLOR SWATCH BOOK

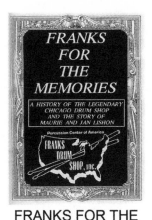

FRANKS FOR THE MEMORIES
History of Franks Drum Shop, Memoir of Maurie Lishon

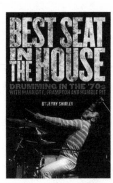

BEST SEAT IN THE HOUSE
Jerry Shirley Memoir

DRUM BADGE TIMELINE POSTER

GRETSCH 1941 CATALOG REPRODUCTION

REBEATS PUBLICATIONS
219 Prospect, Alma, Michigan 48801
www.Rebeats.com